Marie Darrieussecq was born in 1969 in Bayonne, France. *Pig Tales* (1996) was published in thirty-four countries, and her second novel, *My Phantom Husband* (1998), became an immediate bestseller. *Breathing Underwater* (1999) was described by Nicola McAllister in the *Observer* as 'a perfect example of her singular style . . . Her gifts are dazzling', while her most recent book, *A Brief Stay with the Living* (2001) was praised as 'a novel that bears resemblance to the best of Virginia Woolf' in *Scotland on Sunday* and was hailed as 'tremendous writing' by *The Times*.

Further praise for *White*:

'Yet another example of Darrieussecq's originality. In less than a decade she has assembled an impressive body of work; short, sharp, intelligent narratives that are invariably subversive and never become intellectually pretentious . . . This is a subtle study of being and nothingness, and its philosophy is well-matched by the landscape and the ghosts that have never left it.' *Irish Times*

'Absorbing . . . Evidence of her consummate skill.' *New Statesman*

by the same author

PIG TALES
MY PHANTOM HUSBAND
BREATHING UNDERWATER
A BRIEF STAY WITH THE LIVING

MARIE DARRIEUSSECQ

White

Translated by Ian Monk

faber and faber

First published in France as *White* in 2003
by P.O.L. éditeur

First published in Great Britain in 2005
by Faber and Faber Limited
Queen Square London WC1N 3AU
This paperback edition published in 2006

Typeset by Faber and Faber
Printed in England by Mackays of Chatham plc, Chatham, Kent

A CIP record for this book
is available from the British Library

ISBN 978–0–571–22388–6
ISBN 0–571–22388–5

2 4 6 8 10 9 7 5 3 1

WHITE

Traces: a trench below the horizon, spreading out over a circle of beaten snow. The prints of Caterpillar tracks, then of shoes; pathways between the buildings, trampling. Narrow tracks (snow scooters). Black spittle (petrol or soot). An esplanade, a kind of centre, smooth and powdery between the empty tents.

It is dawn. Dawn lasts a long time here.

Two centimetres of snow since last year; not enough to wipe out the traces. No one left in a radius of four thousand kilometres, except for three Russians who are hibernating in the Vostok base. And us, of course, but how can we be counted?

The sea is smooth – in other words (as Edmée Blanco learns in the on-board manual), almost still, with wavelets. Waves under 0.6 metres. There is 'rough', 'high', 'very high' (waves of eight to nine metres) and even 'phenomenal' for over nine metres. The jab of Scopolamine, against sea-sickness, is itching beneath her ear. Was she right, was she wrong? You had to get injected before setting off, it works on the inner ear, and when the sea is calm, the loss of balance is so great that she is moving about like a child learning to walk, staggering, hanging on to the furniture. The crew make fun of her, this drunken woman in the midst of upright men. They, of course, have not taken any Scopolamine, barring that impish character who rolls his own cigarettes. She has spotted the trace of the jab beneath his woolly hat. Concentrating on reading the manual has made her head spin. Its lines drift around, mingling, breaking space into cubes. How about going out on deck to get some fresh air while she still can? Tomorrow, the temperature is going to plummet and the swell rise, waves will surge across the deck – or so the Moldovan sailor tells her in his English from the ocean shoals, as he wobbles and bulges before her eyes (will she get the last laugh thanks to the Scopolamine?).

Lying down is even worse. The motor is like a piston in her bones, the joints of her skeleton vibrate, her flesh can hardly keep up – especially her stomach. Flip over like an octopus. A stink of dampness and diesel. All the same, they have been very good to her, with this specially revamped luggage compartment, now that there is a woman on board for once. Push your shoulders into the solitary recess, feet forward, sit up and bang your head. But she prefers this to the bunk beds in the dormitory area. On the other side of the partition, it is like a bear pit in a frenzy. Some of them have asked to be strapped down for the entirety of the crossing. Which bunk will roll, and which will pitch? That was the question last night, on leaving the port. Look. There's rust blossoming on the ceiling.

Singapore. He had not realised that there would be a stopover in Singapore. He is not dressed for the season at all, not for an equatorial climate. The uniform anorak is just perfect, in fact. He did not want to go into town with the others. So ten hours spent waiting in the airport. The others all changed their currencies into Singapore dollars – a stereo, gold, diamonds, computers and even a holocam, and the girls of Singapore too, no doubt. Some go there just to get the visa. *Tap, tap*, the stamp on the passport. *I was here, I was there.* Blue palm trees behind the bay windows. A litany of international flights, *ding dong. Passengers. Flight. Number.* Fluttering blue palm trees behind the window. Conditioned air, almost cold. The equatorial palm trees sway and tremble, must be at least 40°C outside. A blustering wind. Trunks wavering, flat across the grass of a fluorescent, surreal lawn. His colleagues are all sweating in their Hawaiian shirts, laughing silently on the other side of the window. As for the White Project anoraks, thanks a bunch.

In a store in the duty-free zone, Peter Tomson idly buys a watch equipped with a chronometer. All around, women in saris, emirs, Sikhs and crew members bustle about, as well as Singapore Airlines hostesses (the hostesses on Singapore Airlines are the most beautiful women in the world).

She sits on deck, back leaning against a funnel. In the blue air, the black and white peaks of Tierra del Fuego are still visible above the highest waves. Then the sea replaces them. Then the peaks are back again. Then the dark, broad hollows of the swell. Then the sea shifts up again, and that sharp mountain air returns . . . Take off . . . Swoop down . . . The Captain motions to Edmée through the window. It is getting rough, the others are already back safely inside – Edmée walks straight, Scopolamine victorious: another mouthful of fresh air before being shut in for the great crossing.

From the crest of the wave, all you can see is the ocean. Here we go. Above the Captain's little geranium on the gaming table, water, only water, and the sky of course, an angelic blue as it tips and turns. In the steward's room, a veteran glumly stocks up on apples, then goes to bed for the crossing. The Imp rolls a cigarette, smiles at Edmée and offers it to her. Well? The non-seasick club of the jacked-up.

Then there is the Captain, of course, and the three Moldovan sailors, and one or two other off-green colossuses who would never admit to being sick. The little geranium, the sole presence of vegetation, sways like a tree in the sea breeze. The Imp (who is a French glaciologist): 'Is this your first time over?' Ten days of sea, cigarette smoke and diesel, she will need a strong stomach. The glasses rattle in their compartments, the plates clack, the tables are bolted down. The Moldovans serve dinner patiently. And the water in the jugs, separate from the main mass, conscientiously finds the right level: poop . . . prow . . . prow . . . poop . . . And we, too, in the glass of water that is the sea, and so on. Or in the guts of a large rodent. The Captain alters course to avoid their first depression. Rely on him. One of the Moldovans is a Russian speaker, the other two speak Romanian, which makes three sailors and two camps. As for the Imp, it is his second time over, he gives Edmée the low-down: 'Things are going to get nasty any time now.' The polyglots in service are starting to bolt steel screens over the portholes. They then ceremoniously tie down the geranium on to the instrument panel.

If Edmée can still eat, then this is definitely thanks to the Scopolamine. The Moldovan sauce keeps the chicken glued down on to the plates, while the potatoes float above, like cosmonauts in zero gravity. Then they flop on to the floor, or mash themselves, according to their angles of trajectory and cooking time. The bench is soldered to the table, which is soldered to the floor. The Russian-speaking Moldovan mumbles something and crosses himself, runs down to the steward's room, then clambers up again, his hand gripping the banister rail. A ballet school, with the mirrors missing. Edmée and the Imp, still spared, smile at each other. But not for long. At the top of the crest, a void.

The stomach, crushed beneath the lungs, is about to spill upwards, a moment of weightlessness – *CRASH*: the ship's belly slaps against the wave. All the body's organs in the toes. A kind of silence. A glazed white light. Under the wave. Then the sea – a black wall shattering against the smallest, as yet unprotected porthole – then the sky at last. Screaming to make himself heard, it is Pinocchio swallowed by the whale's maw. The ship screeches, the engine can no longer be heard. 'Rolling is worse' (the Imp) 'You can anticipate it when it pitches, but you just endure it when it rolls.' Edmée nods slowly, so as not to vomit. Only three survivors left around the table, plus the pilot up there in his – cockpit? – and the Moldovan who resignedly clears the table while making long involuntary leaps. Water and wine mixed together, potatoes flattened. Tobacco, diesel, nosh. Goodnight to the Imp.

The floor shoots away from Edmée's feet, she gallops – the boards are trying to grab her – then she struggles up the stairs. *Bang, bang*, seize the handle, the metal cage of the corridor and the stink! The floor criss-crossed with puke. Brown paper bags hooked on to a railing, a Moldovan explains by putting his open mouth above one of them, *BAARRF*. Got you. A ghastly sludge as far as the toilet door, potatoes and chicken, don't look. Floor up, floor down. In the bowl, muddy water and lumps swell and recede . . . The siphon compresses it all, pumps air from the starboard side, and the sea from the port side, gurgling and spray – Jesus!

Get up and step over the entire row? Claustrophobia. Dry heat. The hypnotic purr of the plane. And the neighbours asleep. Peter half-raises the blind of the window: a blade of sunlight cuts through the plane, a sabre – the sleepers grumble. Below, red Australia. Near the front of the cabin, other passengers unsheathe their swords, too: noble paladins! Morning light in aircraft, the rolling planet shifting the night from one shoulder to the other, liquid day in the dense air. Unfold yourself for a piss? Stretch your legs, Economy class is hell, one cubic metre for an entire body, legs folded in three, elbows in your ribs, lungs compressed. Down below: not a single road, or farm, or green patch – the second most arid desert in the world – the first being Antarctica. Red fabric with black rips in it (canyons? landslides? fissures?) and then plumped up in places (hills? rocks? mountains?). Watching out like a kid for kangaroos.

Slowly, they draw near. In plane and in ship. We contract ourselves. We make room, we create space by making ourselves scarce. The appointed zone feels all the emptier. We hear one another rustle, movement is already movement. What language will we have to speak? It murmurs and starts to percolate through us. A game or two on the ice. Five suns, look, up there! And for no one.

That foul water has soaked through into her socks. Curl up in the sleeping bag, inhale a little eau de cologne from the bottle (burning whiffs, orange blossom). Strap yourself down firmly in the bed. Head . . . feet. Feet . . . head. Your guts do a flip . . . stomach squeezed beneath the diaphragm – then in free fall through the intestines . . . The ship flops down, *crash!* Turn out the lamp. Scopolamine, let it go. The instant of suspense at the crests of the waves becomes almost pleasant. This ship has held up for thirty or forty years now. Fine. (A former tug. A pig-headed little tug with a double, flat-bottomed hull: solid stuff.) Being rocked a bit vigorously, that's all. You knew what you were getting yourself into. No going back now. And just as well. It is hot. Someone is swearing in Romanian in the gangway. The sounds are in place, violent but regular. The repeated shock, below the hull, a booming gong and splintering glass. The *ta-ta-ta-ta* of the engine (concentrate on the bass notes). Metallic creaking, ship, sea. Friction from the water, bubbles, the sea unrolling all around . . . Let it rock you . . . Hear the earth drift away . . . rest . . . sleep . . .

The air traffic controller of the Alice Springs region introduced himself, his voice travelling with the plane at five hundred miles an hour, which is quite slow when compared with the globe that is shooting along below, so he introduced himself, gave his directions, the Captain entered the data into his computer, and the plane swerved twelve degrees east, with a slight shift of its wing. The sun was now entering straight through the few windows with open blinds and the sleepers were wriggling, their numbers falling as the air hostesses start to serve breakfast – and later, when the control tower in Woomera takes over (fifteen degrees south, a humming of automation, liquidity of the air, the pilot adding two degrees extra to avoid some cumulonimbus, and so it is without perturbation that the air hostesses can gather up the breakfast trays), Peter Tomson does his breathing exercises. The air is thin, but never mind, *just a glass of water please*, wouldn't touch another drop of that coffee if you paid him, concentrates on his breathing, the dawning sun straight on his profile, the red soil still in the shadows, twenty-four hours' travel already and Pete Tomson is stuck in a window seat, trying to relax by doing his morning yoga – low breathing, stomach slightly puffed up, his sides raised and his clavicles back – and meditates,

9

his eyes closed, concentrating on the space between his eyebrows, the *point of knowledge* as the yogis say, emptying himself, his body unburdened, aware only of his breath flowing in and out of his nostrils – and we ghosts, the companions of long-haul aircraft, contemplate him.

Edmée's mother explained that it was a custom, precisely one hundred and one days after death. The whole family congregated around the square fountain. *You can't do that!* For Edmée, what mattered more than anything was her reputation on the estate. At the windows of the buildings, her mother and various members of her family are applauding. There are even cameras filming. The oldest women, the mourners and the creatures that have always had beards and uncut nails, tear at the earth with their bare hands. The four little coffins arrive, immaculately white and clean with their gilded metal handles. Her mother pulls her by the elbow and drags her back home – a dark coolness while the barbarous ceremony is being conducted: with fine scrapers, the shreds are removed. The perfectly clean, bare bones are then put back into place with the skill of a jigsaw-puzzle master. 'Thank heavens we still have this little treasure,' her mother says, breathing in grandmother's eau de cologne. Edmée hears her words in the faultless multilingualism of dreams – a shock more violent than the sea wakes her up, and that word lingers on her tongue, *treasure*, and the sensation of the dream melts into the folds of her brain.

Sydney was broadening out around the cockpit, while Jan Perse and the Finn twisted round their heads and stank (perspiration) leaning down over Peter (flat suburbs of Sydney, stretch of sea and skyscrapers in the distance); and while the next row (the Queen Mum, the medic and

Claudio Brindisi) were asking for more wine because it was free. In the cockpit, at the centre of the world, the Captain and co-pilot had switched to manual with the nonchalant seriousness of men in uniform, each watching the other's movements, as the rules require, in a relaxed routine, the ponderousness of skill, jokes zigzagging across their lips and Sydney broadening out, the ground gradually becoming vaster than the sky, unequal hemi-spheres between which the plane, *crack boom*, lowers its landing wheels, *two thousand feet, one thousand feet*, then faster, *five hundred, four hundred*, and faster still, *fifty, forty*, and at top speed, *ten, five, four, three, two, one*, the synthetic voice was not programmed to say *zero*, which could bring bad luck, the sound of tyres breaking the shock is sign enough that all is well – while we, crammed together behind the pilot and co-pilot, or sitting on the nose of the plane, or curled up in Peter's armpits, we embrace each other with our ghost arms and, for a second, *thump*, delight in the sensation of touching down.

Peter Tomson stretches, has had enough of this has Peter Tomson, thirty-something, heating engineer, born God knows where but naturalised Icelandic, of parents who had adopted a local name (or rather, their idea of a local name), Peter Tomson is there, crammed up against the window, with a desire to run a mile, and wonders (in the language of thought) what the hell he has got himself into.

It would only be said over her dead body that Edmée Blanco had ever missed eating breakfast. Unstrapped – *clang* on the metal partition – then kangaroo-wise, from one section of the wall to the next, she allows herself to be drawn along the gangway full of vomit to the dining room, where there is only the Imp and one of the Moldovans left, and of course the Captain on his bridge. Just three drops of coffee at the bottom of the cup if there is to be any chance of you managing to raise it to your lips. 'Even the coffee tastes of puke' (the Imp). The smell is everywhere, the portholes bolted shut. They are in a closed Tupperware bowl being shaken like mad. A strange grey light, the light of the sea, alternates with the whiteness in the washing-machine portholes. They are not being submerged by the waves any more, which is already quite something. 'In three or four days, it should be calm' (the Imp, with a disgusted look) 'My sleeping bag is full of sick from the upper bunk, no one had time to run to the toilets, or even open a paper bag.' Edmée turns towards the porthole (in other words: swivels her buttocks on the bolted-down bench while hanging on to the table): black bubbles, then a spiral of water, then day-light – horizon askew, overhanging waves and a grey empty sky – then the spiral of water, sea, bubbles. Under the water, in these depths, at these latitudes (the furious fifties, soon the polar circle), what creatures are there? A giant squid's tentacle sticking itself, *splash*, against the window? 'Mermaids,' the Imp suggests. 'Just dry toast for me,' another Frenchman says, sitting down courageously. The cups in their metal compartments, *cling . . . clang . . .* the coffee from one side to the other. 'When I think' (the Frenchman, livid) 'that some of them are coming over by plane! BUNCH OF POOFTERS!' The Imp rolls a cigarette, lights it. The other just has time to stand up, they hear him running and cursing along the gangway; a terrible din of gastric plumbing. The Imp smiles at Edmée.

Edmée Blanco, telecommunications engineer, thirty-something, born in Bordeaux, France, residing in Douglastown, an estate near Houston, Texas, married to

Samuel, a NASA administrator, is authorised to go and see the Captain. The bridge is the largest area in the ship. It is also the one with the most beautiful view (and right now the only one). Despite the sheets of steel protecting the side windows, there is still enough windscreen left to get a good look at the sea, stretching wherever you turn. The sea with its gaping maw. Black blades, head on, rise up and crash down, divide into the same number of black blades that rise up over even more blades, sometimes decked with whitecaps (attack them side on, down again – admire the Captain's skill: beard, hairy chest, pectorals, eyes of steel and Captain Nemo's ghost leaning over his shoulder).

Edmée Blanco is interested in the radio system, and makes it understood that she knows a thing or two (she is not there as a tourist, but on a mission: like everyone else, her place on board is justified). The sea rolls on in her field of vision, her retinas constantly relay to her brain the sky, the sea; the sea, the sky; grey, black; images which it then decodes and the Scopolamine stabilises. 'It's getting calm' (the Captain, soberly). Rain bubbles are being thrown against the windows. Southwards, we can see an anticyclone that is starting to swell, and further still the icebergs, which the ship's instruments will soon detect (the passengers of the *Titanic* draw away in disgust, with a faint murmur). Whales, two miles off. Squid in the deeps. Great schools of giant cod. A little Twin Otter aircraft above the clouds, heading for Terra Nova, and two albatrosses gliding across the waves: here they come, enormously slow, crossing their trajectories beneath the poop. Edmée has never seen such large birds before. And if her brain does fill with interference, images of tricycles, swings, green lawns and a fountain, then it is not because of any lack (on our part, at least) of attempts to entertain her.

Peter Tomson, after a flight of thirty-six hours (not counting stopovers, and three changes of plane) is asleep as the little Twin Otter finally lands its skis on the Antarctic snow of Terra Nova. It slithers onwards. Stops. The Queen Mum, Jan Perse and the Finn look at one another questioningly: let him sleep. In the greenhouse, where Peter is having an exhausting conversation with his father, roses are growing in great quantity.

Singapore, Sydney, Christchurch, and now this place. Windows white with frost. The pilot refuels, long coils of pipes, like a service station by the sea. From his father's mouth, words emerge in curls, like outgrowths at the foot of rose trees – what are they called, the green shoots that will never bloom and consume all the plant's energy? – *click*! with the secateurs. He is stuck with this idea instead of finding the right words to make him shut up. Always the same dream, what a con trick sleep is, one of nature's messed-up functions. Always more tired, more vigilant, on waking up.

A decision is made at last. Do something at last. Reply to the ad, and there we are. And what if he got off for a while too? A hot drink would be nice. Sore throat. No bars, of course. The fat guy, the Queen Mum, motions to him: sea lions, just great. It looks like a camp site over there, beyond the sea lions. But which way to go? A good two metres away from their teeth. No idea how fast these beasts move. The Finn comes back with some Coke, die rather than drink that. Plus his digital gadget bought in Singapore, to bring back holograms of the penguins for his kids. Sure he hasn't

14

looked at anything *outside* the eyepiece. Sore shoulders. Sore throat. And his mother coming into the greenhouse, or Nana. Or someone else? A figure through the panes of glass – who cares?

A hot shower, and bed. Going to have to wait a while. Another few hours' flight, to the centre, to the Pole. It's enough to freeze them off. You can't see anything through the windows. Where else could you go anyway? So make your mind up. It could have gone on like that for years. Shackleton, the real hero of the Poles. Not like that butcher Scott. Shackleton, the real gentleman. And the rest of them obviously know why they are here. Salary tripled, or quadrupled. Bonuses. The distance, cold and risk. Adventure. As for the fat guy, he who cannot be ignored, it is his fourteenth season. The cook. It must be more exciting than being shut up in the depths of a restaurant.

What will the heating system be like? Just hope it starts up again, after that we'll see. When it's below zero in Iceland, people are cold like everywhere else. They must have given him the job just from hearing that word Iceland, even though heating systems up there are based on hot streams, steam and volcanoes. The Gulf Stream, geothermals, people have no general knowledge. Just hope the thing starts up . . .

Spilt Coke – no, not *spilt*: petrified instantly, *scritch!* A little pile of brown crystals, never seen such a thing. Don't touch anything metal without your gloves. Their security rules . . . it was as if (when they took him on) they imagined that such things were second nature to him. Iceland, the magic word! The fat guy, the chef, always get on good terms with the chef, the next down from God, and Jan Perse, the maintenance manager, they're all bosses, in fact; what about him? He's the chief heating engineer, up to

15

him to warm them all up – they're banking on him, be careful. And they're expecting a woman along, apparently, the radio operator, the burning subject during the flight. *Try and laugh at their jokes a bit. Stop pulling a face, make a social effort. Exhaustion, that dream – just hope things will be all right, down here . . .*

Black, slow, limp sea. Why so black? The depth, perhaps. People are starting to re-emerge from the ship's belly, survivors from the bunks. They hail the Captain from the bottom of the steps, *hello, bonjour, buongiorno*. They are hungry (the Moldovans groan). Little by little, the swell changes its angle. Their bodies sway, incongruously, disconcertingly, sideways, like crabs. The Imp and her are the champions. The sea no longer has any flecks or notches, but a sort of ample smoothness that swells, then contracts. The horizon is a hazy strip between heaven and earth. Impossible to see where the light is coming from. Where is the sun, what time is it? (eleven a.m. New Zealand time). An acrylic sky. A uniform, opaque greyness, extremely matt in the distance, with perhaps the underside of a cloud sinking into the sea: a squall, or something white (like a tooth, a sail)?

Iceberg! The Captain has his binoculars glued to the window. Childish steam from noses on the pane. Edmée no longer knows what to look at or where. On the screen of the sonar: a large mass, quite near; then looking up she can see it, there, her first iceberg. White and clear against the blurred sky. A horizon at its base, traced out neatly on the black sea. Hard to gauge its height. Ten storeys, thirty storeys . . . And very, very long. Occupying the entire breadth of her retinal range: white on white, and flat, and parallel with the sea – a ribbon. The Captain lends her his binoculars. Black sea/red blotch (geranium)/black sea/grey zigzags in the sky/and there: the white wall. A clearly sliced piece of cake. Icing sugar heaped on top. Thin horizontal strata passing across the binoculars. Bluish shadings here and there, overhanging. And towards the bottom (white/blue/white/blue flashes) the blueness of a deep fracture. A sort of cavern. As blue as . . . blueness itself, as the unknown? Nothingness? Fear, for sure. And the Great South.

It is a scout, a sentinel. A warning. Something enormously white. And imagine how cold it must be, in the centre. It is not something that warms up the deeper you go, like the Earth, or bodies. And behind it, the impassive continent. You can imagine that if you went around the iceberg (how long? an hour's voyage? a day?) there would be the hidden side of the moon, signs that have been left there, an intention. But this has nothing to do with humans. It can do without them. Ice, that's all there is to it. No meadows after the thaw, or trees, or streams, or even familiar deserts, with sand, scrub, a dried river bed. A *wadi*. No, that is all meaningless. Edmée would like to believe (a sentinel, an emissary) that it is on the look-out, waiting. That it wants something of them, and not just nothing. A piece comes away silently. An upsurge of spray. 'Big as a washing machine! As a thirty-three tonner! As a house!' The bared ice is amazingly blue. As if, inside this white thing, dwelt the colour blue. As if its original pigments ran there, and melted. And as they mingled, they gave birth to the grey of the sky, the black of the sea. The incessant beat of that light, not white nor sea nor sky. If she tore off a lump, would it be blue in her hand? A blue sun, a cold sun. *And we're going that way, it's this kind of continent that I'm heading for – retrace your steps, go home, back to the drawing board, why take things so much to heart? Nothing of this is any business of yours.*

The cross-shaped shadow of the plane moves on and nothing, nothing interrupts the whiteness: no crevasses, or riverbeds (*wadis?* what was he expecting?), nor, for example: dead trees, trunks, animal skeletons? No oases, of course, no stones. A completely deserted desert. Flat, a little hazy if you really try to focus on something. No horizon. A pale blue sky and white ground: in between, something like atomised air. The Finn is taking photos through the window. The light: a permanent dawn. Maybe that's what he's photographing. Like it is back home, in Karelia, or God knows where. (Russians, in any case. Finland – the arsehole of Scandinavia.) Peter Tomson is pleased to be in the middle, between the Finn and the Queen Mum. Trying to lose as little heat as possible. Hasn't remembered (or failed to listen to the instructions) to put on his shell boots. He has his wool-and-silk socks, his thermal gaiters and his Gore-Tex shoes, but not his shell boots. And he is freezing from his feet up. Herzog. Lachenal. *The first up Annapurna 8,000.* Especially Lachenal: '*I do not owe my feet to French youth.*' A man, a real one. The hero of the entire business, and a gentleman to boot. But all this does not warm up Peter Tomson's feet. He wriggles, as people do at such times. The very idea of having to cross the entire cabin to get to the baggage . . . of stepping God knows how over his neighbour, of struggling with the frozen lock of the trunk to get his shell boots. Why not conceal his ill-shod feet discreetly beneath the Queen Mum's ample calves?

And it is up to him, Peter Tomson, to go and re-ignite, to restart, to service the generator on which the entire Project depends. Water. Heating. Electricity. The incineration of shit and waste. And he will have half an hour to do it in, not a minute more: as a precaution, the pilot will not turn off the engine of his plane, and if retreat does turn out to be necessary, periods of stable weather are extremely brief. Everything has been codified, planned and drafted with thoroughly tested security routines, even for the least likely set of circumstances. Elsewhere, the substance of the world is hazy. Here, everything has been defined. As a rookie, he prefers not to think about the procedure in case of failure. His predecessor gave up after two seasons, despite the bonuses. To be on call, twenty-four hours a day. Woken up at any time by the breakdown alarm. Once the season is under way, with everyone on the base, the restart time goes down to twenty minutes – the time it takes the water to start freezing. Failing that, it is the evacuation procedure. Everyone knows what to do. Take as few possessions as possible and shut yourself up in the survival chamber. Wait for help to arrive. Apparently, you can hold out for months there. Or a year, if need be. While listening to everything cracking up on the base: the plumbing first, then the machines, and so on. But this has never happened. At least, not to the Europeans. It seems that the Australians had to evacuate once. But that was not necessarily because of a heating problem, there are plenty of reasons to evacuate. But it is hard to find out about such things. *Top secret*. During his interview: *it is only at the South Pole that the profession of heating engineer reaches its apogee.* He thought they were taking the piss. They are getting nearer. What's the temperature in the cabin? Minus thirty degrees C? And outside: minus sixty?

The pilot is now flying low across the snow, at an altitude of five, ten or twenty metres (it's hard to say, with no

19

points of comparison). Won't they crash into a pylon, ha ha
ha. The Finn starts wriggling beside the window. Without
losing an ounce of his dignity, Peter Tomson turns his
head to get a better view (a cold blade on his nape). A red
ribbon, separated into little blocks, small bricks (*Lego*)
topped with black smoke: the expedition's Caterpillar
vehicles. 'Fresh food!' says the Queen Mum. Peter murmurs sarcastically. But feels bad at once. What on earth
does he know about the taste of tinned food which has
been piled up on the base winter after winter? The little
convoy provides some sense of proportion through this
strange fog. The Caterpillars hoot their horns, and the
Captain hails them with a right-left shift of his wings: the
Queen Mum collapses on to Peter Tomson, who collapses
on to the Finn, who bounces back off the window, *bing*.
Serves me right, Peter Tomson thinks. Supposing that eternal justice exists – an idea that would have made him
laugh if he had really thought about it, but the tribunal of
signs has been present inside him ever since his childhood.
He wriggles his toes to check. Lachenal's ghost leans over
him: all is well.

'Quite an ice cube, isn't it?' (the Captain). Edmée hands him
back his binoculars, the blue/white wall shifts away from
her. Visual re-adaptation. Distances. The sea. The iceberg
grows, the entire horizon vanishes, or nearly. (One-tenth
above water, nine-tenths below. What you can see, and
what you cannot. The marvellous predictability of the
physical universe.) To the naked eye, the surface now
becomes clearer, cracks can be made out, and that extraordinarily pure blue. At what depth does its massive keel lie?
It moves slowly, freed from its glacier, on its way . . . drifting on the currents, only stopping when it has melted (in

ten years? a hundred? a thousand?). Higher and broader as they approach, and the humans smaller. The laws of perspective, in fact. How many houses? If the skyscrapers of Houston were erected on it, what height would they reach?

And the White Project. The construction of a permanent European base at the heart of Antarctica. For the moment, people only go there for a *season*, during summer (the easy life at minus forty degrees C, instead of minus eighty in winter). They live in prefabricated huts and tents, which are as well heated as possible. First, logistics arrive: five scouts aboard a Twin Otter. He, Pete Tomson, along with the project manager, the maintenance manager, the site manager and the cook. According to the shipping rota, they will soon be followed by the much talked-about radio operator, the medic, the chief engineer, and a few others, including a handful of glaciologists. Are things heating up right now? Everyone wants to know. Then, the Caterpillars will bring along fresh food and the workmen. But, first of all, Pete Tomson must get the main generator working again. He wriggles his toes.

'I'm going to fill her up!' (the pilot). The plane nose-dives, Peter's guts rise up to his lips, as he sees the sparkling ridges of snow, with their granular crust. Only Laplanders or Innuit would know the precise term in their native tongues for this nuance of snow, and shade of white. But here, no one has ever been born. The plane zigzags, regains altitude, descends once more. They're looking out for the tanker. The tanker that was left here by the previous team. Pete Tomson reconfigures his mental projections: we are not going to land at a petrol station, we are not going to have a cup of coffee, we are not going to warm up our feet while lorries, *crash whoosh*, make the bay windows shudder. A tanker, then. At the front, Claudio and Jan Perse are staring out, beside the pilot. It must be covered by just a fine scattering of snow. Bright red beneath the flakes. *Crack boom*, Pete Tomson slams into the Queen Mum, while the Finn, forewarned, takes the shock against the window. *Ratata-ta-ta-tap-tap*, the propellers slow down, the plane lurches and stops with the shiver of a hovering dragonfly. *Here we go!* The pilot elegantly grips the top of the door then leaps down. Pete Tomson painfully unfolds himself and goes after him, while the Queen Mum curls up – 'the door!'

We, who haunt the tanker, are definitely all present. Our last visitors date back to the previous season. The pilot has connected the nozzle of his petrol tank to the valve of the tanker. He pumps, and coolly lights a cigarette. What Peter looks at first is the red tip of the cigarette, the only hot point in the universe. No problem with vapour, of course, how stupid can you get: it is so cold that there is no smell of tobacco or of kerosene. Or of anything else. IN CASE OF EMERGENCY, CALL 938 000 00. It is an Australian number. The Melbourne Fire Brigade. Capital letters on the red tanker. It brings a smile to Peter's lips, and a great void in his chest. He glances all around: everything is empty and white. An immense plateau of snow. It is hard to breathe, the altitude is about 4,000 metres. A round dome, a continent of accumulated ice. Can you call that a landscape? With a clear mist, at a man's height, as if the ground were evaporating directly into the atmosphere by sublimation. The liquid state is unknown here without human intervention (the heating system, restart the heating system). A low, pale yellow sun. Long blue shadows, the plane sketched

22

across nothingness, hardly a trace of its skis, and that white, immaculate, infinite crust. The pilot's soft, steamy, orange profile and, at the windows, the childlike faces of the Queen Mum, Claudio, Jan Perse and the Finn. The *tap-tap-tap* of the slow propellers. This odourless, insidious pollution bugs Peter.

We surround the tanker and watch it emptying, with a sucking noise from the pump. This is the sole event at this point on the globe. Tanker full/tanker empty: the passage of time, a few snowflakes here and there. The convoy of Caterpillars once a year. The sun setting in splendour for nobody. And it is night for six months. Then the sun rises, dawn lasts for weeks, pink, green, yellow, and in its final gleams, the first plane lands with four or five humans. And there we are. Six months of summer. It has been the same pilot, a former American serviceman, for the last fifteen years. He yoyos across the continent. He particularly likes landing here, in the middle of nowhere. And always, as he fills up, he relishes his cigarette in the cold, with the pronounced, precise gestures of the living. We would so like to play a trick by hiding the tanker, burying it, siphoning off the fuel, sabotaging it, but the large amount of energy required for such games would no doubt empty us out, too. Pete Tomson has put his orange anorak over his dry-suit, the White Project uniform – *I can't stand uniforms, but you have to admit it's good quality material* – a double layer of Kevlar and real down. The pilot's gloved hand passes across his field of vision, it rises to his lips, grabs the cigarette and, opening his thumb and forefinger – lets it go. The butt follows an almost straight trajectory. Its temperature drops by ninety-three degrees C in under a second, it hits the ground, rolls for three centimetres and stops. The traces of saliva have already frozen. A thick rubber sole (the pilot's shell boot) automatically crushes what remains. The filter falls apart, with pale Virginia tobacco, ash, paper. Pete Tomson bends down, removes his right glove (while the pilot is slipping his own glove back over his mitten) and, one by one, picks up the scraps and remnants. It takes five hundred years for a filter to degrade in a reasonably humid climate, so you can imagine that it will be preserved for all eternity here. What to do with it? In his anorak pocket. There are few scraps of ash left, Peter tries to bury them under his heel, but the crusty snow (whose name a Laplander would know) is extremely hard, and his toes hurt. There must be the pilot's butts at all the places the tanker has been positioned. And the kerosene vapours and cigarette smoke stagnating there. *Ratatata*, the slow propellers go. Pete Tomson suddenly feels all in.

But his torment is not over yet. While the pilot is disconnecting the fuel pump, the Queen Mum opens one of the windows and throws out a plastic bag marked *Castrol*. A slight wind rises, who would believe it? The sun's rays swerve about, curling up, refracted by the ice, on the rebound. Crystals glitter, in suspension. The light shifts about in strips, as if we were blowing it through silver floss. But Pete Tomson cannot appreciate the show. The propellers have already accelerated (whirlwinds of frost), the pilot is looking at him from behind his dashboard, everyone is looking at him. Pete Tomson is running after the plastic bag. Claudio, Jan Perse, the Queen Mum, the Finn and we ghosts change sides in the plane to get a better view. The bag, closed by a knot, is as round as a football, and the wind is pushing it across the hard snow, *screeeech*, the green and red logo flashing in the white air.

24

Enclosed in the bag, the Queen Mum's urine is cooling by five degrees C per second, and at this instant has reached the consistency of whipped cream. When Pete Tomson, out of breath, leaps forward and manages to grab the bag in its flight, its contents shatter in his hands.

The orchestra was playing and the bird-headed violinist was watching her over his red scarf. The louder the din got, the louder he played: with strident sweeps of the bow at each crash. And he was smiling at her: *All is well, all is well. Nothing of this is any business of yours.* Yet those explosions were making her heart leap and when she turns round: terror grips her breast like ice. The iceberg has devoured the entire prow. It keeps coming, with white blocks falling away. On and on and on again. Over the rigging and over the orchestra, *bang crash!* She is in the pit and, all around her, the musicians are playing through the avalanche and the crashes, the bird-headed violinist louder than the rest. Cracks and frost!

Out of breath, in a cold sweat, Edmée Blanco sits up in her night-dress with a start. The noise – the one from the car breaker's yard behind the estate, with that huge crusher which squeezes and compacts, what jaws! – she puts on her anorak, as though slipping on a dressing-gown, and tiptoes barefoot between the mounds of sick in the corridor. The ship gathers its strength again and again – bracing itself as though attacking a particularly steep wave, a moment's pause, hanging there – *crash!* – then a brief whistling fall. In the steward's room, it is seven o'clock, New Zealand time (but what does that mean in their location?). People look at her with curiosity. Lots of new faces (are there that many passengers on board?). Sure enough, it is rocking far less. *Crack, screech,* a strange lurching but one which can be anticipated more easily. They are even eating bread and butter. So Edmée climbs up the ladder to the bridge, because she has permission (the privilege of ladies and those who have not been sick) and sees:

A white sea below a white sky. The sea is covered with ice, undulating in sheets. Split by black zigzags. A supple marquetry, with occasional raised forms, cornices, heaps, large ice cubes turned over, *splash!* Over there, to port, the water is still free, as black as leather. But – the Captain explains – what with the relative thinness of the pack ice, and the good weather conditions, we will continue straight ahead. He looks pleased, does the Captain. There is laughter from the steward's room. And the Imp? He is outside, in his Project dry-suit, which he has unpacked especially. They are about to attack the pack ice, aren't they? At first she has problems singling him out among the groups in orange uniforms, leaning on the rails, as though on a cruise. A whole crowd seems to have emerged from the bunks, as if the holds had hatched out their eggs and cocoons. That old film, *Body Snatchers*, which she saw with Sam on the estate – going so far away and with so many people points Edmée's internal imagery in distinctly gloomy directions. At least with this weather they are going to be able to open the portholes and air the place a bit, for heaven's sake. Downstairs, they have probably all got their eyes fixed on her legs but: look over there. Something on the ice is moving in a strange way. It is not a block of ice. It is organic. The recognition of the living by the living. A seal.

The ship approaches. The seal looks asleep, its ribcage rises and falls. A living place, a warm, breathing place. Where its head or tail are you cannot tell for the moment.

The sheet of ice it is slumped on is also rising and falling, indifferently. Blinding in the sunlight, with this creature at its centre. Edmée is dying to ask for the binoculars, but does not dare make herself any more conspicuous. After all, she is in her night-dress. Finally, it waves its hand, or paw, in the air. *Hello, hello*. Or else, *hey, I'm here, look where you're going!* They draw nearer. Straight towards the seal. 'A petrel!' someone yells. A white bird, found near coast-lines, has crossed Edmée's field of vision while she was watching the seal. You cannot see everything at once. 'Soon, the continent,' the Captain announces, Christopher Columbus-style. The ship is approaching the seal, and Edmée Blanco starts getting worried. Has the Captain seen it? And the gestures it has been making? The prow rises, a great mass of metal, *splash!* falls down, the ice cracks, it will make a pancake out of the seal in no time. Edmée Blanco would rather the expedition did not begin with a murder.

In Pete Tomson's dreams, we are like we are in the cine-ma . . . in the modern cinema of holograms. Across a dis-torted landscape, upright shapes stand out, concretions of lava that solidified long ago. Peter's mother is holding a chisel and making the shapes ring like bells, *ding*. She leaps across crevices, vanishes occasionally, and makes the depths of the fissures ring, *dong*. She reappears: in one bound, she crosses the streams of lava. The geysers of boiling water that surge up from the glaciers cannot touch her, *pfut*. A bounce by the plane – if planes do bounce – or rather, a brutal right-left shift of its wings, throws Peter Tomson once more on to the Queen Mum. What's going on? Claudio Brindisi, who is bored, is pass-ing round some photos of his wife. Peter realises only later on that they form a striptease: Mrs Brindisi in her dressing-gown, Mrs Brindisi in a negligée, Mrs Brindisi in a pair of . . . of lace shorts? Before seeing the end, Peter pretends to go back to sleep. If you focus on the plane's engine, it produces a never-ending sequence, a high note followed by a profound pause, a *taaaTAtaaaTA*, which is pleasantly regular.

'What let Scott down were the ponies. I mean, ponies in minus forty degrees C! Amundsen won thanks to his dogs.' Like everyone else, Jan Perse converses in international English, his nationality remains uncertain, but Pete Tomson reckons that he is Norwegian. 'Scott was an utter prick' (Peter, suddenly taking part in the conversation). The bleeding wound in England's heart splits open again inside the Queen Mum's, and he takes a deep breath to protest. 'So was Amundsen,' Peter concludes, closing his eyes again. (Scott and Amundsen, sitting on their spectral arses, look jointly offended. The ponies eaten by Scott whinny with vengeful laughter. Meanwhile, the dogs scratch their fleas in limbo.)

The Queen Mum's laughter shivers out, Jan Perse is talking loudly. Mrs Brindisi's red thighs are walking through Peter's neuronal circuits. He tries to chase them away. An image pops up between two pieces of fleshy interference: a geometry of shadows; something is there, at hand's reach, beside him, he recognises it, but it fails to materialise. A scrap of a dream. A bubble from the ocean's depths, briefly rippling the surface then popping – its contents dissolve in a fleeting glimmer . . . It belongs to him, reminds him of something. He knows that if he found it again – just its colour, a shape, a word, a tiny part of an image – then the entire film would begin and the dream would unroll like a ball of wool. But that would take an enormous effort, and Pete Tomson just lets himself glide away elsewhere.

They were getting used to this new, marine rhythm: the leap on to the step of ice, the crack, then the fall. Lying on her bed, Edmée Blanco was letting herself be rocked by the forward surges and breaks and that moment of absence: *chchch . . .* when the ship's prow slid into the thickness of the ice. You could count: 1, 2, 3. They were suspended for about three seconds, one crocodile, two crocodiles, three crocodiles – the little Higgins girl had taught her to count like that, in units of crocodile-time. So, despite the distance, she could still make use of that lesson here: the knowledge of the Higgins children, the knowledge of the estate, of the fountain and of the swing – anyway, this moment of absence – this sinking into the ice – was quite unlike the gulches in the swell. No seasickness, but you could still become intoxicated by it, rocked to death, be incapable of getting off the ship again . . .

We ghosts are having a whale of a time. Smooth rollercoasters, ghost trains . . . Lines crossing before Edmée's eyes . . . Time passing by so easily, hop, crack, *chchch . . .* There is a small library on board: *Hunger, Moby Dick, The Sun Also Rises*, the diaries of Scott, Amundsen and Shackleton, Ibsen's complete plays, an ageless collection of *National Geographic* and, strangely enough, a small book for children in French, entitled *Mon petit doigt m'a dit*. The tale is based on the idea of secrets being revealed. On each page, the boy's little finger whispers to him what his sister, parents or nanny are hiding. And an illustration, decked with lightning bolts, depicts each revelation. Who can have left this book here? In the maze of holds, a clandestine passenger – a child locked *clang!* inside a container?

29

And she alone had a clue to its presence on board? Edmée Blanco shoos away these ghost flies. She rubs her nose, like when she was little. At least there won't be any insects. In the end, that was the clincher. There are already all those spiders in Texas, thanks a bunch, and those massive roaches which survive insecticides while spinning around like tops . . . Of the two small ads – the erection of a new satellite aerial in the heart of Guyana, and a simple contract for a telephone operator in Antarctica, which was well below her qualifications – she chose the Pole because there are no insects there. In Amazonia, the creepy-crawlies are monstrous. And up, and crack, and *bzzzzz* . . . plus forty degrees C on one side, minus forty degrees on the other. No chance that a single fly will survive. They call it the austral summer. For the Mars mission, it was already too late, after the mice, dogs, monkeys and clones, the human teams had been selected long ago, and anyway she did not have the right qualifications. All through the interviews, that tyre-swing in the play area in Douglastown squeaked in her head. What was Antarctica like? ANT-ARC-TI-CA. The Arctic is the North, just a huge pack of ice; but Antarctica has a bed of rock. Were there meadowlands in summer? Migrant birds? Herds, some sort of bison? Like in Alaska. Igloos. But everything extremely cold, all the same, nice and clean and chilled.

Hanging on to Edmée, we ghosts are having a whale of a time. And up and crack and *ziiiiii!* Leaping from thread to thread, the swinging spiders of her thoughts! – Leaning over the rail, and up and crack and *chchch* . . . With the same curiosity, we watch the rigging start to freeze. How quickly this lace of frost has been embroidered! Then the coats of ice, the stalactites-hang-on-tight of frost on all the instruments on board! – Through its transparency you can make out the hatchways, cleats, lifelines – in the coats of ice, the enveloped ship turning turtle! Like a bone in skin that has turned translucent, and don't we love it! The continent nears, the temperature falls, the still, icy air is increasingly palpable on the human skin . . . And we, hanging on to the rail, and up and crack and *chchch*, like bats, heads downwards . . . in the hiss of the frost as it hardens . . . Because, if we want, we can view the film speeded up, forwards or backwards, in slow motion, the film of the approach, the film of the ice, the film of time solidifying here like ice. In the whistling of the water trapped in the rigging, even more audible for us than the rhythm of the ice-breaker as perceived by the living. We can let ourselves be rocked in time to the frost: imagine the power to make the rigging turn white.

The generator is a red block as tall as a man and built like a safe. Go past the on/off button made of black plastic, and the control screen on which a small needle, *bleep*, should leap into life soon if all is well. Lower down, another screen for pressure. OK. And an external thermometer showing minus forty-two degrees C in the tiny shelter. The brand is a well known one, *Caterpillar*, a logo on red enamel. The Caterpillar company seems to make just about everything. Pete Tomson takes off his gloves and emerges from the top of his dry-suit in pullover sleeves and wool-and-silk inner mittens. Face to face with the generator. So, he has half an hour, and a minute has already gone by. Calm it. Panting, pulse racing – it's the altitude. The others are waiting in the plane: there will be no help from them. Breathe in twice through one nostril, then twice through the other. Breathe low, from the stomach. Recover the centre. OK. *Flap-flap-flap-flap* from the plane, a

31

deathly silence in the shelter, you can hear yourself breathe. In this little space, called the Boiler Room. Claudio opened the padlock for him, before getting back on the plane (who on earth would possibly want to break in?). Graffiti on the red enamel. Illegible because of the frost that has peeled away the surrounds of the inscriptions, like scratches. OK. If his sweat gets as far as his pullover, then it will stink for the rest of his stay. Horrible thermal underwear. Is there a laundry here? But washing means water. And water means melted snow. And melted snow means the generator. OK.

Unscrew the four bolts and remove the hood. A galvanised interior, the cold piercing his silk inner mittens. Put at least one glove back on. Now that I think about it, we have got intermediate mittens too, like garden gloves, wherever did I put them? The crank and *thud*. Nothing. A bad contact. Five minutes gone already. The starter. The frost must have . . . The two wires: red and black. OK. Reconnect them . . . Nothing. It must be deeper down, right in the innards. Beneath the arc behind the circuit boards. Like a vet operating. Never seen so many connections. What's this thing for? Did the Caterpillar boys make that? With those blue pipes all wrapped up around the resistors over there? . . . In clumps? And these kind of, of three-way bypasses, never seen anything like them before. It must have been bodged up by the previous guy. To increase the surface of contact. With aluminium tape. He was an aluminium tape fanatic. What a mess . . . he's tripled, no, quadrupled the circuits. Not exactly a pretty job, but with his signature, in a way, a personalised job. He must have been really scared that the pipes would crack. If I took them all out, the tubes, screws, plates, terminal blocks, conveyors and bunches of wire, if I took the time

... to rearrange it all ... then I might come across nothing at all. Fuel. Eleven minutes already. Here's the water reservoir. So that's the fuel tank. The cap's stuck like hell. Even with a spanner. Hit it then, *clang, clang*. Frost. If the oil has frozen (impossible at minus forty-two degrees?) (but if the paraffin has crystallised all the same) – is the carburettor blocked? – if there were two of us, we might still make it. But calling for help doesn't seem to be the way things get done here. Scott. Amundsen. *Schlip*, there it goes, it's opening. He closed it like a thing possessed. Almost full. The oil looks liquid. Fourteen minutes, thirty-seven seconds. It sounds like they've got out of the plane. Stamping their feet like cattle. What's that noise? Like voices. Stamping their feet, a herd steaming in the cold, like little Icelandic horses. Motherland, my arse. Sixteen minutes. Breathe from the diaphragm, one ... two ... I'm going to try to take the time to ... to siphon off the fuel tank. Remove any lumps. If the paraffin has crystallised, then it's obviously blocking it. Wipe down the sides of the tank carefully. After stripping it all down. Then filter the oil. Yes, that's what I'm going to do. There are dozens of jerry cans around here. If this stuff worked last year, then it has to be refined enough, hasn't it? But last winter's cold. Does paraffin remain in suspension after being reheated? Never thought about that. What were they thinking of, that we get temperatures of minus eighty degrees C in Iceland? And the rest of them chatting away outside. Come on, get on with it. Twenty-two minutes. The *flap-flap-flap* from the plane, getting more and more distant, as if the sea was rising ... filter ... pour it back ... Fucking hell, twenty-six minutes. Wire. Starter. Nothing! Kick it ... *BANG! BANG!* The others outside will think they're hearing things. Because of the cold, like optical illusions! And these

33

accelerations in space-time – twenty-seven minutes! Just as well they left the engine running, in three minutes' time we'll be out of here, with the White Project abandoned . . .

RrRrRrRrRrRrRrRrRrRrRrRrRrRrRrRrRrRrRrRr

A mighty heave from the mechanism, the generator snorts, like a horse unleashed in winter . . .

GgnGgnGgnGgnGgnGgnGgnGgnGgn is just about what can be heard from the other buildings, to which will be added a universal glugging as soon as the water starts to circulate.

But, twenty metres away, the silence remains unchanged. We ghosts can vouch for that. Among us, for example, a pioneer smiles as he leans over Peter's shoulder, or else the inventor of the heating system, or else the aluminium tape fanatic: someone who is concerned, whoever, depending on their other commitments, a link in the chain, rushing in, a shadow. Fleeting moments of density in our mass cause laughter to ring out haphazardly. It does not take much to hold us here, in this zone, it does not take much at all. Vacillating, yet perpetual. Solid as ice. In the perpetual whiteness where nothing ever happens, the White Project forgotten. In the whiteness that suits us. Several mythologies situate us here: sometimes we are the dead, or those who are still moving. Above all, we avoid being counted. Of course, we can drift up to the surface of the planet, like an atmospheric phenomenon, El Niño or La Niña, but if the Earth holds us, then Antarctica is our . . . what? Our anchorage? Leave that to the sailors. Our territory? Leave that to the animals, the seals, whales and penguins. Our field? For the gardeners. Our empire, our realm? For others still. Our country? What a joke. Marshland is for the will-o'-the-wisp, lava for trolls, forests for elves; but the South Pole is our identity, like the sea for the melancholic, the *chaise-longue* for the consumptive, or an empty room for the amnesiac. And if precision were compatible with our nature, we would say this: Antarctica is our geographical equivalent. We would set down this equation: that Antarctica is to Geography what our bodies are to History. And we would add that for this *season* (as they put it) we shall certainly be drawn to floating around the White Project. Perhaps even more than usual.

Its rhythms, its maintenance, its moods: Pete Tomson spends the rest of the day checking out the generator. Never mind about the word 'day', when the sun does not set. What is certain is that, at the same time, up, crack, *chchch*, Edmée Blanco is breaking the ice and advancing towards Pete Tomson. Little by little, just quicker than the seals, *hurrumpf*, on their fore-flippers, and a little less fast than the king penguins on their webbed feet, *click clack click*. Of course, Edmée Blanco does not know that she is advancing towards Peter Tomson. No more than he does, either. We alone are ahead of events, we alone are able – if we are so gifted – to plan in advance our observation posts around their point of contact. And, silently, we encourage them (of course the ship was advancing, of course its direction was preordained, of course the ice was breaking, of course the small ads had been drafted and read without our help, and without us the bases and projects were being blueprinted; but as for the fear of insects, the attraction of nothingness, the taste for escape, the boredom, clumsiness, haunting and phobias, as well as the desires, panic attacks, dramas and treasures that build up or fall apart in the long term, we can consider that we are responsible. We get

35

involved in them with the sheer brutality of the thoughtless, as the salt of life mingles with the sea.)

In order to modify the course of an asteroid that threatens the Earth, humans do not send up rockets to destroy it, because that would create millions of small, uncontrollable projectiles. Instead, by gentle touches, as in a game of cosmic billiards, they strike at objects and alter their courses gradually. And so do we. We proceed tentatively. In front of the heating system, two childhood memories burst into Peter Tomson's glacial mind: those recurring little horses, and that overheated school, full of blond, incomprehensible children. The sun shining through the windows, everything is yellow, and those blond, incomprehensible children form a circle around him. They are joined together at chest height by a single Siamese pullover: an Icelandic sweater knitted in the round over a cacophonic breast. – With the horses, it is different. The earth beneath their hooves is mauve and orange. Little Pete Tomson, who has not escaped from the national sweater, is gingerly giving them some bread (or carrots): their muzzles are damp, their teeth large, but they have delicate lips. Their heads (thick manes, small intense eyes) are at the same height as his. When they approached him, they neither walked, nor trotted, nor galloped: they came at that fourth pace which has made them equestrian celebrities. Naturally moving their legs separately, like bipeds, but as if they had grown a fifth one. Anyway. Peter Tomson likes to think that this is his first memory: those small horses, and the carrots or bread which he is holding out on the flat of his hand, just as he has been told to do – who by? He is making this offering with delicious apprehension, and their muzzles are soft and damp (large teeth hidden behind). When it has been accepted, there is a moment of peace between human and animal, between extended muzzle and open hand, that absence of any trap – yes, Peter likes to think that this is his first memory.

Aged six, which is late for a first memory, but such things happen. (There is also something green maybe, a very long time ago, before Iceland, but this recollection is hazy.) At that period of his life (arriving in Iceland, the school, the horses) Peter Tomson is completely mute, even in his mind. The words 'carrot', 'bread' and 'horse' arrive later on, in Icelandic of course. One of his very first words is 'the Indian'. Pete Tomson does not look Icelandic. That classroom, blindingly sunlit, is surrounding him with a single hand-knitted pullover which is calling him 'the Indian'. Later, in Reykjavik, a girl he goes to bed with tells him that if this marvellous world-wide melting pot continues, then tomorrow's man will look like him, Peter Tomson. Completely nuts. A genetically pure, hand-knitted Icelander. All of them dangling from the branches of their family trees, drinking aquavit from period skulls dating back to a time when his ancestors . . . never mind. Small, genetically pure horses, moving in their unique way. Steaming in the cold of those landscapes of sulphur and moss. Before long, his schoolmates also start calling him the Loony, or the Headcase, or the Mongol, because he cannot understand anything, or because he looks so *oriental*. He does not know.

A caddy full of different-sized golf clubs, pulled by a little boy of the same name, wearing shorts and flip-flops on legs as thin as putters. And those absolutely green fields stretching away endlessly. Clearly, this cannot have been in Iceland. There is almost no grass in Iceland, and thus no golf courses; and when they make children work, it is in the interest of society at large. What is more – if this really

37

is one of Pete Tomson's memories – the angle of vision is extremely low, passing just above the caddy, then abandoning itself in a haze higher up. And, in this upper region, there is a red shadow, just above his head, Peter's head – if it really is him, if it is possible that it is him there, his body, his own little body, swinging above the golf ball, his little hands clutching a golf club. A parasol, held by who? By another caddy? It is hot, and lovely . . .

We could almost linger comfortably in this image, relishing its calm, this enigma, this domesticity. But Peter Tomson has finished examining the generator and is rubbing his greasy gloves together. The temperature is beginning to rise. It has been so cold here that the energy being released is visibly vibrating, slightly distorting space. The others open the doors, wipe their feet and converse in loud voices. The plane rumbles its engine before leaving again, empty, the snow creaking beneath its skis. Peter Tomson stretches his cramped legs. He wants a cup of coffee, there must be some around here somewhere.

At that very moment, Edmée Blanco is landing on the coast. It has been morning for some days now, a dawn stretching itself out, pale yellow, orange tints on the sea, pink on their faces. The sky dilutes its filaments on ice and flesh. The fluorescent strips on their dry-suits are on fire, the words WHITE PROJECT shimmer on their backs. Across the omnipresent snow, Edmée's and the Imp's long shadows have red stripes: reflectors on their knees, elbows and shoulders. Their shadowy hats also reflect the sun, like two little flashing lights, swivelling, discovering, commenting; all that is missing is the emergency siren. Here are a few huts dating back to the glorious years, and a village of converted containers, this is where they are going to spend the 'night', then tomorrow, if all goes well, they will fly to the White Project base aboard a small plane, which acts as a shuttle. Wheeled cranes unload the ship: a small scene of dockyard agitation. But what charms Edmée most are the penguins – *king* penguins, the Imp corrects her. The to and fro of humans at work creates a slow tennis match, followed by their beaks, right . . . left . . . King penguins are terribly humanoid. You have to see them, making their decisions together, hesitating from one foot to the other, consulting each other in earnest, with their tiny, hyper-active arms; until the first in line makes its mind up and the rest – no shoving! – follow it into the water. When the young are born, they stand on their parents' feet, insulated from the cold. What father, what mother has not at some time walked with their children on their feet, step by step, as a twofold biped? One parent fishes, the other sits, turn by turn. The fisher parent vomits its catch into the beaks of its partner and young. The scene brings tears to Edmée's eyes. When tragedy strikes – killer whale, storm, exhaustion – the widow(er) would rather die on its feet than abandon the young. Wouldn't it be more sensible to slip away for five minutes and try to fish nearby? But – Edmée would have been told – if penguins have a brain, then it should be seen as a communal one, shared between the ten thousand bird heads that make up the colony.

And so the Imp rattles his bell and explains the lives of king penguins to Edmée, and she, delighted, laughs. She has a mug of steaming tea in her hands, the air is mild on the Antarctic coast, among the animals; she raises her face to the sun, and is happy to be there, she mimics the penguins, laughing as she waddles. We ghosts surround her, envelop her, and if we could, we would caress her. But she is thinking about Samuel: and Samuel appears among us. Samuel in the kitchen, Samuel at the swimming pool, and even Samuel naked, very close to Edmée and out of focus. It is as much as we can do to get rid of the swine and bring Edmée back here, where we are being born. It is from here, the place where she puts her feet, that we might be able to coax her to move on, because the drift of mental continents is our business. Luckily enough, there is the South Sea, and the low sun, and perhaps also the Imp; and then, if need be, rising in the offing, the irresistible spray of a whale.

The long, dark channel opened up by the ship is already turning grey, recaptured by the frost; and what we can capture of Edmée's memories is growing slippery and grey too, would fit into the pigments of a handful of old photos. In the brilliant light of the winter garden, she is playing Lego. The photo is extremely off-centre, towards the left, and this is how Edmée pictures herself: next to the frame, with a large space beside her. It was her mother who used to take the photos. Did she have a squint, or suffer from some neurological disorder? The album is full of furniture, bedrooms, back walls, wardrobes, sometimes trees; and about half of Edmée Blanco. With a bit of luck, as far as the roots of her second bunch, all of her neck and almost an entire shoulder. The life typical of Bordeaux in the 1990s can be seen in the photographs Edmée's mother took: a turquoise, translucent iMac; charcoal-grey linen curtains; a 16:9 television set; shelves of video cassettes; but above all nothingness, a hazy nothingness, as if it were possible to photograph such a thing.

We ghosts know that nothingness is visible only when it is hazy. Because if you ignore the sticks of furniture, which

40

are of no interest to us, and also, for the moment, Edmée Blanco too, nothingness is what can be seen: that is to say, the molecules of nothingness, the whorls of nothingness woven by the dust, the lines of circular lights, the iridescence when the background is coloured, and generally speaking a sort of powder or mist floating around, or rather beside, Edmée. As if her mother wanted to capture something other than Edmée, something greater, or larger, or more elusive, more mysterious; or something immutable; in any case, something that is not there. Edmée to the left, playing Lego in the winter garden. Edmée to the left, smiling with half a brace. Edmée to the left, blowing out the five candles on her tenth birthday cake. Edmée to the left, on something like the wing of a flying saucer, then the rest of the roundabout with planes, motorbikes, sledges and horses.

The house around Edmée is enormous. There are no photos of this house in its entirety. Only the parts that have just been mentioned. The winter garden is her favourite place. A vessel of light, furnished with Turkish rugs on teak floorboards. The garden, the real one, stretches out in front, between two ivy-covered walls. Edmée is allowed to build across the entire surface here, including the rugs. It is a sort of non-aggression pact between her and her mother, to avoid having Lego everywhere in the house. Her mother takes care of the home, and her father is a doctor, an anaesthetist to be precise. It will only be several years later, in a daydream, that Edmée will think about this precise job description, put together the bits of sentences that she has overheard, and understand why they have to leave: a murky business, a patient who had slept until they died. So, in Vancouver, there are no photos, because her mother stayed in Bordeaux along with, among

41

other things, the camera, the television and the iMac. But her memories join up again, clear and coherent: the basketball club, Cyndi and Firouzeh, the Liz Phair concert at The Snowball, and Samuel, and the trip to the Niagara Falls, and her university degrees. As far as the family is concerned, Edmée's grandfather is still of this world, in a rest home apparently, and it is to take care of him that her mother has stayed in Bordeaux. Around the middle of the 1960s, Edmée's grandmother drowned her children like kittens before slitting her wrists, and Edmée's mother escaped only because she was the youngest and with her nanny. What a small thread life hangs on, Edmée's life, and that is what attracts us ghosts, even though her mother told her that it was none of her business.

We ghosts particularly like the house in Bordeaux, and Edmée playing there. The plastic Lego bricks, red, yellow, white and black, with their green bases to act as foundations, the hinges for the little doors, and the chamfering to close the roofs. And then the open spaces all around, beyond the walls and windows: the sky, the seasons. If there is one thing Edmée hates, it is having to go down to the cellar to fetch wine: one of her father's educational notions with a view to toughening her up. The switch is a long way from the door. Nor does she like going up to her bedroom on the top floor: you have to cross in front of the music room. There is not a trace of an instrument there, but the faces of fauns in the half-light. In Vancouver, there will be neither cellar nor music room, and her father apparently drops his educational notions. She can remember the meal on the plane: cubic food, perfectly fitting into its little tray, and the kindness of the hostesses. Anyway, what interests us ghosts is the following point: while little Edmée is flying over Iceland on her way to Vancouver, she knows nothing about the linguistic traumas or equestrian emotions of Peter Tomson, ten thousand metres below her. But this is nevertheless the very same Peter whom she will meet twenty years later, at the heart of a continent about which at present she knows just one thing: it is the white patch pierced by a metal rod at the bottom of the luminous globe which she has had to leave behind in Bordeaux, because it was too bulky to fit into her luggage. That is all.

From these years, there are precious few salient points in common: the fall of the Berlin Wall in early childhood; a film by Captain Cousteau about how sharks sleep; and a total eclipse of the sun. No matter how trivial it might seem, the film by Captain Cousteau is the most stable of these memories. Peter has retained the picture of a cavern full of grey-skinned torpedoes; and Edmée the idea that for the first time we know where sharks sleep, not in the middle of the sea – as was thought – but in the shelter of a lair. As for the Berlin Wall, Edmée remembers the televised images of young people partying and straddling it; and Peter, a Chinese man standing in front of a tank. Years later, he realises that he has obviously been mixing things up, but this is the image which keeps coming back. As regards the eclipse, it was partial for Peter and total for Edmée, because they were not living on the same latitude.

When, one evening in Vancouver, Edmée listens patiently to her father giving her the basic low-down on the reproduction of mammals, she does not know that, at the very same moment, the only little boy with frizzy hair on the entire north coast of Iceland is discovering that the sound of a whistle makes horses' pricks grow larger. But such coincidences are rare, alas, we should so like to have gnawed them to the bone. In general, while Edmée is yawning behind the ergonomic desk in her bilingual

Canadian school, Peter is asleep in his little bed – such is the time difference. While Peter is sweating with panic and trying to memorise the words tumbling from the mouth of his blonde teacher, Edmée, in advance in time, is hopping merrily across the fifty-four channels of North American TV, which already has the cable. And when Edmée marries her Samuel one fine, bright spring morning in Vancouver, Peter Tomson, at last Icelandicised, is managing to decipher the words, or at least the intentions, of an enterprising blonde student.

We ghosts never tire of such obvious facts: that before knowing each other, Peter and Edmée did not know each other at all. 'A quarter of an hour before his death, he was still alive': that is the way with us ghosts. A quarter of an hour before meeting, Edmée Blanco is in the Twin Otter tirelessly admiring the virgin snow, while Peter Tomson is relaxing at last in the video room and watching (for the second time already) the only film he considers worth viewing among the blockbusters and the skinflicks – they still know absolutely nothing of this imminence, even as their trajectories converge. When, pushed on by boredom like everyone else, Peter finally goes out to meet the newcomers (*flap-flap-flap* says the plane in the sky), a deep-frozen Edmée is mentally counting her toes and wondering what is in store for her, but neither more or less so, and perhaps even less so, than those who generally land here.

That is what enchants us ghosts. Such innocence about the curves of time.

It is one long day: with a dawn, early light . . . the sun
coming up . . . executing its circle . . . dipping again slightly
. . . rising a little higher . . . during a good fifty human days,
pink and orange.

Then it stays suspended: North, East, South and West,
around the white zucchetto. The sky is pale yellow, faint,
blue at the zenith. This lasts about a hundred human days.
Then the curve deepens, becoming each day more sinusoidal, and the sun finally touches down, sinks, vanishes,
and it will be dusk.

Then, night for several months, while it is day at the
North Pole. That is how things work, on this planet.

We linger, we like to take our time and stretch it out. To
gather together here, in this slack instant. To recover our
limited strength, to stir up our diffuse bodies. To relax
what we call our eyes, to exercise our diminished senses.

In all, five creatures from the great depths get out of the
Twin Otter. Huge, flippered feet, massive dry-suits,
upright cylinders with two stumps and tiny, dazed heads.
The plane's propellers whip up the powdered ice and a
long lock of hair escapes through the barrier of the balaclava. Only by this lock can you guess that Edmée is a
woman. She could otherwise be a man of average height.
But all of them, Peter included, identify and search for her
curves beneath her White Project dry-suit . . .

Nothing welcomes them here. Nothing wants them

here. The ice swirls, the whiteness triumphs. Edmée has arrived. We retreat a few human metres back: nothing left. In this state, which is ours. We melt into the whiteness, if anything could look like a melting into nothingness, if anything is to be fed, or watered in it, or in us. In this instant of marginal time, when the plane has landed, when the sun is suspended a few degrees from its zenith, when what passes for night is but an infinitesimal variation in the light – a screen of gauze, cloudless – not a breath, nothing happens. Projecting ourselves to the North, the South, the East, the West: nothing. Time curls up. Space is lost. A sinusoidal sun. Set fair, the loop rises, spins . . .

A magnificent light, for them. Rays beaming in horizontally, a stained-glass yellow, white nave, cupola of the sky, the cross-shaped shadow of the plane. And the music of the spheres, *zim, boom*, while they move on with their long shadows, raising the snow. The bottle of champagne in the Queen Mum's hands – *crack!* – suddenly splits in half lengthwise. Welcome! *Bienvenu!* Deep frozen! They shake gloves. The Imp cracks the usual joke about the contract the Queen Mum did not read, thinking that he was being employed in a normal sort of place. Edmée shivers, feet cold, she greets them – *I'm going to spend six months with this lot?* – she wants a shower, a hot drink, she sucks a lump of champagne between her gloves, and Peter looks at her through the dark blue sunglasses of the White Project . . .

In the chemical light, as though between two thin sheets, the filaments, sparks and shapes pass by, in Edmée's eyes the cones wander and the rods congregate . . .

Splashes of liquid sun . . .

Edmée Blanco pulls up her gloves, sucks her lump of champagne, the air is very dry, her heart is pounding, she

46

is out of breath, it is because of the altitude, she had been warned, and that odd smell in the air, and this fat man smiling, holding the two halves of a champagne bottle, and him, over there . . .

She is panting, looks nice, she is not used to it yet, all the newcomers are panting, in fact, he hopes that she has been warned about the altitude, the slither of air going in and out, her lips already dry, already cracked . . .

(The White Project sun cream, the White Project lipstick . . .)

Him over there, looking at her from behind his dark blue sunglasses, saying nothing.

We have encountered many travellers before stopping off at this moment: Cook, Weddell, Scott, Amundsen, Shackleton, Dumont d'Urville. Of course. But those before them, too, those who talked of the Terra Magna, Terra Incognita or Terra Australis. And ghost ships, and so on and so forth. One of Amundsen's companions, who died of typhus, is weeping on the deck of the *Belgica*. One of Scott's men slips into the icy sea – his cry, every night, recurs for the crew of the *Terra Nova*. The bottom of the world, the pivot zone, the meeting of curves, the crucible of magnetic fields, here, everything is possible: impressions, noises, fatigue, thawed objects, states of mind, blown-up ideas, the end of worlds – muttered conversations, when the living quarters are thick with smoke. Coughs and yawns, the smell of feet and the odour of meals over a last drink. The stories of the Finn, the site manager, his eighth season already – pickled and cured, red eyes, blue skin – and they call us ghosts! . . . That you can hear a baby crying. Cattle bells. The halyards of boats trapped in the ice, continuing their voyages through infinite spaces. And the cohorts of shades, in silence, like uprooted nations. The traces of their footsteps when they wander away from their camps, in long, inexplicable lines. Beneath the perpetual sun, this perpetual weariness. Conjunctivitis and panic. Crystals in suspension, reflections, hallucinations, mirages.

Let us allow Edmée Blanco to arrive, without mentioning the vodka and the excess. The boredom and vague dreams. The failed hopes, the fantasies. And all the things humans bring here, with us slung over their backs. It is the whiteness, too. The absent horizon, lifted away from the ground. The ground and sky now uncertain. But they do not dwell on such matters, avoid awkward subjects, nothing about the anxiety and cravings, about the distance and the madness, about turmoil, nothingness, the desire to kill and the fear of dying, *in case of emergency* the first aid comes from Australia. Or else break the glass, ha ha ha! Apart from us, the nearest contacts are three thousand kilometres away, on the coast! Do you think they talk about claustrophobia on Mars? That they crack jokes about previous missions that have failed? And the nightmares you have in the rocket, when you manage to get some sleep? *Vast is the kingdom of dust.*

Weight and lightness are things we have forgotten. What were breathing or asphyxia like? Two bodies that come to a stop instead of crossing through each other? And not this mess of limbo, no interpenetrating halos, no poltergeists, no vague smirks or that changing-room atmosphere, jokes about the Queen Mum and this enclosed space. What about the others on the base? Some distant love stories – not that they fail to bring them along, but what interests us are their bodies. The resistance of flesh. What happens, at this instant. To start with, the snow being crushed beneath their soles. Water evaporating beneath layers of textile. The skin, teeth, lips, toes, mass. Bodies standing on the Earth, which is turning fast enough to hold them there, and slowly enough not to crush them. Peace all around, and the air they breathe, and food for months, ice in large quantities and an excellent generator made by an American company to melt it and keep them at thirty-seven degrees C. The necessary conditions. And us, focusing our strength on remaining in this second, neither too far backwards, nor too far forward; trying to stay here, to see and to capture. We are floating. We are looking for balance. Suspended in time.

They retreat inside the buildings – *I'm going to spend six months in this place?* – canvas and sheet metal (those of us who pass through walls sigh). At that second they see each other. Whether Peter keeps on his dark glasses or not . . . Whether the particles of light that convey Edmée's stare have to cross that barrier or not . . . All the photons emitted by Edmée's shell shoot in a straight line on to Peter's retinas in order to reconstruct an image of Edmée, with the memory of light. And with just as much infallibility, her optic nerves inverse the image, left to right, and the lobes of her brain put it back the right way, *zig zag*, and here he is, Peter.

Wide open spaces! Teamwork! Personal commitment! The spirit of adventure! Amundsen! Paul-Emile Victor! Captain Cousteau! Captain Cousteau's red bobble hat!

Edmée is listening to the welcome speech in her orange fleece, from below the hood, where she has hidden her hair, her nose white with sun cream – even that makes her recognisable as a woman – none of the other humanoids here present has sunk so low as to use sun block . . .

Is she going to take her fleece off? Isn't she hot like that?

Several of them are wondering about that, but Edmée is apparently concentrating intently.

Is he going to take those glasses off? What's he doing keeping his glasses on indoors?

And we dance on this thread, as we wish, we are in our element, the in between: the isocentre of Peter and Edmée, this very point of contact: seeing each other. A thinking, fleeting substance on the thread of their gazes. We dance for a second, then Edmée looks away, no doubt wanting to listen to the speech, and Peter does likewise, wanting – apparently – to listen to Claudio's speech all over again, always the same, the precautions when using the incinolettes, whether to use toilet paper or not, what the Antarctic Treaty has to say about waste, concerning each person's role and team spirit. Time to break ranks.

Intense emotions weary us. We are not very mobile, it really takes a lot to move us. Despite what many people think, it really does take a lot. We do not budge for no reason. We, who survey the continents. Who wander wearily across eternities of snow. These zones of space with no use. Snow, crystals, the sky, suspension – us, absorbing time. Time being absorbed here, right here. This is what suits us.

It is more difficult for Edmée Blanco to get used to this nothingness. She sometimes takes a stroll around the base, in an attempt to understand where she is. No, not to understand. That is incomprehensible. But to sense – like migrating birds? – this geographical position, this distance, this solitude. To feel this nothingness in her body and mind by concentrating on it. Compass, radar, GPS: the brain lacks instruments. But there is the imagination, instinct – try to grasp the depth of the snow beneath her feet, several kilometres of it, and all around her, as far as the coast, several thousand kilometres. In either direction, tens or thousands, width or depth, it is just as hard.

She could try to imagine infinity, like she used to do when she was little, because the mental effort is just as daunting. Add on ever more distance and depth, and more at the end, and more whiteness to the white. On the surface, it is imaginable. After a certain time, after the snow, there will be the coast, and the pack-ice, and the open sea, then the three lifebuoys of the Earth: the Cape, Tasmania and Tierra del Fuego. And, if you continue, the arcs will finally join up again, like wickerwork, up there, at the North Pole.

But the depths, beneath her feet: the tons of snow, the eternal ice and the pressure that liquefies the ice, creating unbelievable lakes of heavy, almost hot water . . . and below the lakes, bedrock as old as the Earth and, as far as we know, lava, a core of iron . . . and caverns of diamonds . . . and more lakes . . . and creatures buried there . . . and out again through the maw of a volcano, *whoosh!* on a spray of sulphur!

The entrance leading to the centre of the Earth is in Iceland. She read that in a comic book. There were six blank squares, where the heroes got lost. They were in hell, and hell means having no up nor down, nor width nor depth, nor right nor left, nor any stable point. To move upside down and feel only nothingness. Inside and out, neither hot nor cold. The Fall of the Wall, ha ha! Of the House of Usher, *c-rash!* In the six blank squares, the lost souls turned about without advancing, trying to find a solid footing, but constantly floating. Here, at least, there was still the ground and gravity, and the sun above their heads, and the whiteness more or less confined to lower down – despite the fact that in the sky there were hazy regions, shadings, vibrations – anyway, there was not that much complete blankness.

51

It was to fill this nothingness that the image of Samuel started to float around Edmée Blanco. And his voice was floating too, as a protective layer of sound. Edmée went for short strolls around the prefabricated huts on the base, the sun white, the sky pale. And she heard: 'Edmée'. Her thermogenetic underwear was itchy, the stitching scratched and sweat was soaking her socks. The old hands knew better: you bring along your usual under-wear, it is quite sufficient and far more comfortable. As soon as she started to walk, the heat was overwhelming, and she had hardly stopped before the cold hit her like a slab. Between two breaths – the air's liquid ice – the cold had crossed all her layers: fleece, dry-suit, pullover, vest, but also her skin, derma, fatty tissue and muscles, her tra-chea became a dry, frozen tube and her lungs went rigid as far as the tiniest bronchiole. Dreaming of the open air, to be alone, quiet, to think things over: it was impossible. After two days, she had to accept the fact that the only place to be alone was with your arse parked on an incinolette!

If you succeeded in distancing yourself a few metres, you could soon take in everything there was to be seen: the prefabricated dormitory, the kitchen, the living quarters, the heating system, the glaciologists' lab, the little radio booth where she presided every evening during the two hours of satellite link-up time, and the skeleton of the future base sticking up – a few metal girders covered with a sprinkling of snow. All the buildings were positioned a few metres apart from one another, to avoid any risk of a fire spreading, which meant that they had to strap them-selves up again in their dry-suits, shoes and shell boots as soon as they went through a doorway. The wind turbine, standing slightly to one side, was the final sign of human presence. It was turning slowly, *chip chip*, on an uncertain breeze. The satellite dish was fixed on its mast. And there we are.

The ground rose up, curving like a hoop – an optical illusion. The horizon looked extremely high, the sky made of mastic, the sun pallid: as though seen from a thalweg. The shadow of the turbine spun incessantly around the base, like a 360-degree sundial. The traces stopped there – but not the smell, the stink of burnt shit. Wide open spaces, my arse. No flush toilets here, each bowl is equipped with a little electrical incinerator, *whoooosh!*, and the shit goes up in smoke. At 2100 hours, Edmée took up her post, firstly for the routine messages, contacts with the coastal base, the weather forecast, despatches, then personal calls. Two hours later, the sun still just as high, the base left the orbit of the satellite and *flop!* silence fell. If you calculated her rate of pay on the basis of these two miserable hours, then this was some cushy billet for Edmée Blanco. But she had come there to think, and she just couldn't.

Or else withdraw yourself, like the Yogi, him there, the Indian, the Headcase or whatever, had apparently managed to do. All the same, Peter isn't exactly a complicated name, it's even cute, can be pronounced in any language. He'd sit there in the lotus position in the corner of the living quarters. At the time when the others get out the booze and the playing cards. It was really daring of him. Breathe in, and out. Despite the smoky air, when you looked at him it was hard not to breathe in and out with him, it was like catching a giggling fit. And he always kept his glasses on, to isolate himself, no doubt. He presumably took them off when he was working, but she never saw him at work. His job seemed to be a particularly lonely one, like a light-house keeper's. The alarm went off, he left without a word, at which point if you prepared to evacuate you'd have looked like a real rookie. Otherwise, constantly in the video room. He was not very chatty, this Yogi, Indian, Headcase. Eating with a disgusted expression on his face. Looking vaguely worried, constantly put out. But he was the one who kept them warm, who supplied them with water, in its liquid form. Just thanks to that, they left the Indian, with his constantly furrowed brow, to his own devices . . .

He removes his glasses, but doesn't look up. He's listening to the Imp, he smiles. Everyone likes the Imp. The world is the Imp's pearl-filled oyster. The bastards are all wearing tee-shirts. It's roasting in the living quarters. But if you move away from the heater, and sit by one of the walls, you'd freeze instantly. A permanent sore throat from the dry air . . . If she dared, she would do meditation exercises like him. This is maybe the opportunity to take up yoga again, after the Higgins tragedy. We're so far away from it all. So, go back to square one. Why not put a mattress in the radio booth, and turn it into an off-duty bedroom? Breathe in, and out. Feel the air in her nostrils, the slight constriction as it goes in, the throbbing as it leaves. Feel her presence on the ground, thighs, buttocks, and her spinal cord, vertebra stacked up, the axis of the planet. Sit on the South Pole and feel herself spinning, *whirr*, a magnetic wind in her ears . . . to be no more than a breath, in and out, the passage of air . . . to be open to the world, just there, anywhere, on burning coals, at the bottom of a lake, in an overheated tent, and think of nothing, not even of not thinking of anything – she used to be able to do that, once.

Was the Yogi making a spectacle of himself in the din and fug of the living quarters? His gleaming, clean, black hair bent down. He could be asleep . . . Smooth brow above his glasses. Blow on his nose, as you'd blow away a feather . . . Would he raise an eyebrow? Eyes open, or shut? Hard to say. Kneel down in front of him, then would he raise an eyebrow? Push back his locks from his forehead. Examine the fine lines as you would read a palm. This is the right place to be telepathic, a good twenty humans together in the middle of nothingness, the only centre of warmth, only centre of thought for kilometres around. To slip from one body to the next in the openness of self-absence. At the Douglastown Community Centre, they passed around the *Om* by touching the tips of their fingers, a long breath in, then a vibration deep down in the throat, and the sound passed from one body to the next, one voice to the next. Except that it always ran up against Imelda Higgins, and that she was always her neighbour, her neighbouring *Om*. Long, red-varnished nails. Their pointed touch against her when, feverish despite the teacher's instructions, Imelda took the precaution of opening her mouth wide long in advance, so as to add her own *Oooom* when the time came. Too many anthems in too many schoolyards, too many hurrahs with the cheerleaders. She used to be a primary school teacher, apparently, before having all those children . . .

Edmée Blanco is starting to feel feverish too. It must be the altitude. Or claustrophobia. All those men taking more or less sneaky looks at her. Mentally, she shifts back from the Yogi. Looks away. Gets her breath back. Rubs her nose. She has work to do, too, and things to think over. She, too, has an important job. Without her, they would be cut off from the world. Could no longer talk to their wives, or see their children. When you think how important phone calls become, in this place. The hologrammer is a pretty good quality one, for a European budget, and it would be silly to

55

under-exploit it just because satellite reception, during the two hours of link-up time, is only barely tolerable. There was something she noticed this morning: a thin layer of frost forms on the dish during the 'night', when the temperature dips with the angle of the sun. The sun scarcely moves, and yet the frost comes back, intact, during the absence of mankind. Edmée decides to scrape clean her dish every morning. It will give her a morning mission.

The Indian, the Yogi, Peter, as you wish, has already left to examine the gaskets in his generator. The alarm keeps going off because of these damned washers. The Imp and the glaciologists are continuing the drilling they started last season. This year, they are hoping to reach three thousand metres before the Americans. Dimitri, the meteorologist, is eagerly awaiting his section of the drill core made of million-year-old ice – a first. As for the Imp, he waits all day for his five precious minutes of satellite link-up time so that he can speak to his wife. The Queen Mum has put on his apron and decided to make Chicken Marengo, with half a bird per person, and salmon tartar as a starter, then defrosted Brie de Meaux and an apple tart *à la Bourdaloue*. Raw vegetables are already getting scarce, alas. But the Queen Mum performs miracles in a place where the little humidity contained in a kilo of sugar is enough to turn it to stone, and bottles of champagne sabre themselves from top to bottom. The Finn labours over the plans for the future base, he is wrapping himself up before going to take a look at the girders. The convoy of workmen should be here in a few days. The medic is on call – but he always is – and is staring through the window at the slow spin of the wind turbine. Claudio is off checking his electrical circuits with Jan Perse, because someone has once again pissed in an incinolette, and the fuses have blown, of course. This evening Claudio will once again have to repeat that you DO NOT PISS in the incinolettes, that you piss in the urinals that have been provided for that very purpose, and that you STOP YOURSELF FROM PISSING when shitting and that you stand up BEFORE incinerating, and once again Edmée will get the giggles.

Every morning in Douglastown, when Samuel had gone to work, Edmée Blanco made the house her personal business. Tidied the kitchen, emptied the dishwasher and put the morning's bowls into it, wiped down the table, swept up the crumbs, cleaned the sink; then the bathroom, then the bedroom. After that, she sat down at her computer and went through the ads to find a job far away.

Not that she imagined she could get rid of Imelda Higgins when going through customs, or freeze her out on crossing the polar circle. When all the world's TV channels homed in on the estate, and Edmée found herself being a witness like everyone else, she was seen on television rubbing her nose, with that gesture that was so typically her, and swaying from one foot to the other, and saying – not very audibly, not very convincingly – that Imelda Higgins was goodness made flesh, that nothing had led anyone to foresee, guess, imagine, and that only the day before . . . which was all untrue, because Edmée (and the entire neighbourhood with her) had been perfectly capable of guessing; it had been staring them in the face. Hence the not very audible bit. Hence her embarrassment when her brief appearance comes back to her. Here, at least, no one saw it. Where the Higgins tragedy is concerned, people want Edmée Blanco. But this embarrassment may well be for her, and for all the others, the only possible emotion left. With Samuel, for example, you could read the embarrassment on his face. While the cameras were still there, while the hacks and sound engineers were still beneath her windows, picnicking around the fountain, Edmée had cotton-wool for a brain – or a heart, for that matter. When she was asked to show her emotions in public – cotton-wool, like the others, on her tongue and in her heart. When the tide went out again, they found themselves alone beside the fountain, with only us for company. Us, and only us, perhaps even more palpable than before, but still us, neither more nor less. The weekly two-hour psychological support sessions were still being held at the school, but the adult programme had lasted only a few days in the Community Centre, and Edmée had not had the strength to go along. Samuel told her that he had cried there and that this had done him good, after that he looked permanently embarrassed. And no matter how Edmée adjusted her White Project dry-suit, or carefully laced up her boots, or cleared her throat and scraped away at her satellite dish, embarrassment was like a gluey snow, despite the flaming landscape, despite that raw light that forms the very landscape itself.

Dressing to go out, taking a turn around the buildings as far as the turbine, climbing up the ladder that runs up the mast where the satellite dish has been fixed – this already takes her a good half an hour every morning. Empty houses, *scratch scratch*, in a normal climate, *scratch scratch*, decay from the invisible effects of rather mysterious forces; here, *scratch scratch*, it happens a thousand times more quickly. As if the ice formed again as soon as human agitation stops. As if the ice re-formed over nothingness. Just as the surface of a lake resettles after circular ripples and a forest after the machete. Well-equipped and hard at it, Edmée can stay outside for a good two hours at a time.

And we ghosts take a round trip from the South Pole to Douglastown, stirring up the dust and the frost.

The sun is as high as it would be on the estate at that time; but it is not the same sun. The Houston region boasts a semi-tropical climate, the sun shines on extremely green grass. And the automatic sprinklers – *chi chi chi chi* – chant like cicadas. Or let us say that it is extremely difficult for Edmée Blanco to believe, to think, to stop for a second and say to herself that this is the same sun. The same as in Bordeaux, Vancouver, Reykjavik or Bombay. The sun in these parts – and any rustic or tourist nuance in this expression should be ignored – the sun that remains constantly above the White Project takes the form of two or three white pastilles standing out on a blue background, vibrating slightly, and generally marked with mauve, criss-crossed lines and rainbow-like shadings. This double, or triple, effect can be explained by refraction of the light in the suspended crystals of ice, and the shaded sun cream in the fingerprints on sunglasses. Edmée was in fact taken on because the previous operator had had to stay in complete darkness for thirty days after his return, because of a detached retina which gave him visions of the Virgin in the form of a blue-and-white rabbit. Anyway, the sun shines in its own way on the desert in these parts.

Every morning in Douglastown, the grass grows *chi chi chi chi* while Edmée struggles bowl by bowl, crumb by crumb, sock by sock against Samuel and chaos. Here, every morning she scrapes the satellite dish. Every day, when the medic checks her pulse, it has slowed a little more, but it is still over sixty per minute. The altitude. The cold. The change of routine, different sleep cycle. Her periods, too, are off schedule. The Queen Mum makes hot tea in a thermos for her little morning excursions. Hot drinks

59

against sore throats. He adjusts her balaclava and pats her back. Scrape down the dish, walk, a spot of exercise. Good daily discipline, like him there with his yoga. It slows the heart rate. And every morning the light is the same, and the great white plateau around her is the same. With a few hollows and bumps formed long ago, waves of ice, sastrugi. Turning gaseous towards the horizon and rising above her, as though in a basket; with us inside, just the same, unchanged.

We sketch out whorls in the frost which Edmée breathes out. Appear, disappear. She takes good long breaths, conscientiously. The dry air stings her throat, but it is pure, very pure, and she has a talent for breathing. The smoke from the incinolettes maybe wafts this far, but it is already so cold that its odour has vanished. The ideal match between what she is looking at and what she is breathing, this is what holds Edmée Blanco. Incandescent crushed ice. Whiteness, frost, and the desert. It is as if Edmée has managed to empty herself out. That beneath the zucchetto of her skull, a toxin-free brain is turning in time with the continent. That, maybe, she has found what she was looking for here: emptiness at the end of the world. An untouched base of the globe.

One sun, two suns, three suns: on the horizon, we raise up mirages. With its faceted eyes, a fly would see something quite different, but we are putting ourselves in Edmée's shoes. In any case, a fly would die instantly here. The ghost of one of them, brought over in a crate of oranges, is buzzing in the spectral ears of Scott's ponies. 'Every day, I feel as if I were drowning kittens,' wrote that murderer Scott, about his ponies. We come and we go. Our comings and goings make prisms in the crystallised air. We assume a form in Edmée's breath then become formless.

Her fingers are cold in her gloves, she passes the wind-screen scraper, which she found among the building site equipment, from one hand to the other. *Scratch, scratch.* Her shadow, like a little chimney sweep, quavers beneath the ellipse of the satellite dish.

The slow spin of the turbine. Shattered blue shadows. This is a place to which visiting humans have given very few names. Not many come here, and none stay (alive, that is); and those who have kept a diary did so to recount their conquest, an exploit, or to say farewell to their loved ones with their frost-bitten fingers. Later, those who will stay here for scientific, political or military reasons will speak international pidgin English and will content themselves with *snow, ice* and *white*, or hazard a *desert* and *flat*, or when effusive *solitude*. And when they are alone, quite alone in their minds, alone with their mother tongues, why would they describe anything? Edmée thinks of the Indian, Peter, the Yogiman, whatever his name is. It is almost outlandish to watch him at mealtimes, doing like everyone else, curling his spaghetti around his fork and lifting it to his mouth. So he does have a tongue and teeth, and even an oesophagus for his food to go down. So he does bother to curl up his spaghetti, he is concerned about everyday things. He wipes his mouth and asks for some bread, yesterday evening it looked as though he was listening to the glaciologists talking about their drilling problems and the quality of the ice. '*Skol,*' he said to the Finn, who was pouring him some wine (because he does drink wine and can say 'cheers' in numerous languages), and when the Imp told a good one, he laughed along with the others. Will he never have a call to make? No family, friends, homeland? Someone to wish happy birthday? We are here for half a year. Everyone, absolutely everyone, has now been to Edmée's booth. Has been on several occasions to Edmée's booth. Because there does not seem to be anything to do here except think about the world you have left behind. About children, trees, seasons and hills. 'White Project speaking! This is the White Project, hello! Bonjour! Pronto! Esan! Diga! Haloo!' Edmée Blanco even tries to say the right words in Finnish. If there is any satellite time left, she goes on the Web to find out how to say such and such, she keeps herself busy does Edmée, she is motivated, except that the Finn is not Finnish, but Estonian, a point his wife Ida, in Tallinn, does not bother to explain to the silly cow of an operator, given the cost per minute of a Tallinn–South Pole communication.

When Edmée looks up, to give her fingers a rest, she can see five suns. One in the middle, and four others around it, linked together by a corona, a white halo, what a blaze there would be if ice could catch fire. Five glorious suns, decked in our veils. Is it any hotter? She feels like taking off her anorak. Can she hear music? Like whale song? A vibration of the spheres, a ripple from the clouds? It is the huge silence, pressing on her eardrums. She would need a camera to be sure that this image was not forming in her own mind, to be certain that she was not going mad already; and a telephone to upload the photograph to Samuel, how ironic to be right now up the only aerial in the vicinity (mind you don't fall). A kind of local rainbow. A polar phenomenon. She will tell him about it: it was beautiful, oh so beautiful. But sad, too. It was sad to be alone looking at something so beautiful. And these adjectives stick like Scott's and Amundsen's flags on Edmée's zucchetto skull. They spark in her ears:

It was beautiful, but it was sad
It'd make a fireman weep buckets
When the bucket was full, a drop dripped out
On to the floor, where it froze.
And the fireman captain slipped over and died
It was beautiful, but it was sad
It'd make a fireman weep buckets . . .

The song her mother used to sing her when she was little, that's right, during her childhood, and there was a different version about a bean – *a drop dripped out on to a bean's young shoot, it was beautiful, but it was sad* – which Edmée's mind tries to chase away (encephalic wall taut as a drum), there is enough interference in this scene as it is. And we sing, all together:

It was beautiful, but it was sad

And Edmée Blanco pictures the red fire engines going by, sirens blaring, the giant bean of the fable growing as well, and that awful news story about a child being suffocated by a bean that had germinated in its nostrils, and the bells of the ambulances and Imelda's red nails, anyway Edmée Blanco stares at the five suns, and her human brain is the sole living thing, messy and living, in all that array of spheres and of crystals.

There should be someone else there to get worked up, someone to yell out: 'Look!' Another body defined by its skin and circulating blood and capable of putting one coherent thought in front of another to say whether such a thing exists or not. Get scared or thrilled with someone else so as to break the spell, the weight, the silence. Is it really beautiful? And by the time she runs back to the base, will it have vanished? The thing in the sky with five eyes is looking at her, Edmée, with no apparent interest. This is no show, it is not an event, it is there neither for Edmée nor in spite of Edmée. It is there for no one, just like the snow, the ice, the lakes in the depths and the bedrock beneath them, like the sky and the tiny hint of wind and empty space. It is expecting nothing. It wants nothing. It is flat, cold and indifferent.

Edmée turns around, but all she can see is whiteness melting into whiteness and, over a few metres, the traces left by her own feet in the snow – Armstrong's anti-skid soles in moon dust. But Armstrong was being followed, step by step, by the entire world's television channels – as the people about to walk on Mars will be accompanied too. Edmée Blanco is turning numb on her ladder. What the hell is she doing here? The central sun seems to be gradually isolating itself, detaching itself from its corona and pulsating on its own; while the other four, like drops of mercury, stretch out the halo into a strange cross with rounded tips; they melt, their light dissolves and turns into the sky, the sky and the ground meld into one. We are dancing in Edmée's eyes. Whiteness is everywhere, as though the molecules of the air were frothing up, and we dance. As though the two-way mirror of space had been flipped over to its one-way side; and the Project, just thirty metres away, had melted away and vanished.

Edmée comes down the ladder. Her enormous boots, right and left. Edmée places them in front of her; she swings her fluorescent gloves in front of her, to pull herself out of this mirage. A sensation of cold in her sinuses and throat, and the quickening beat of her heart, that is all there is left for Edmée, all there is left of Edmée. But something is now twisting the air in her ears – a real, shrill ringing – something is happening. Peter Tomson zips up the top of

64

his dry-suit hastily; he can see Edmée standing motionless in the whiteness; and of the twenty minutes he has, he uses one minute twenty-five seconds to grab her arm, hold the door open for her and wait for her to go back into the warmth.

So we move away, we roll up our veils, one single sun now pierces the white fog and we curl around one another, just as cats curl up in humans' houses, and Peter works and the alarm goes quiet and the purring of the generator starts again.

Pete Tomson's eyes are wide open. The worn-out Velcro on the door flaps lets the sunrays in. And some still air, motes of white vapour . . . It is so . . . so beautiful outside. A speckled sun through the tent canvas. How do the others manage to sleep? It is 0141 hours. The heater is in the middle of the dormitory; he is terribly hot, especially his feet, and his throat is dry. If you turn it down, two minutes later you're freezing, and that is no figure of speech: in this place, it's work flat out or die. How do they cope in the spaceships to Mars? Maybe he should have applied for a space mission? Pitting yourself against minus 100 degrees C, that's really something. Warm up Mars. Do they take women up there? That strange fog yesterday, they call it a 'whiteout', the sky reflected in the snow, or vice versa; and the space between them is shut off, wiped out . . . She looked lost, on another planet. A metallic, blinding mist . . . Or else, think about those lakes, for example. The idea of lakes beneath the polar zucchetto. That was interesting. He had never heard about that before. Lakes of pressurised, liquid ice, well below zero, but liquid, and increasingly dense as you go down . . . imagine it: the warmth of ice. Lying on his back, Peter Tomson dreams on. His throat now feels less dry, his insomnia less unpleasant. His neighbours' breath is less fetid, the lack of comfort can be forgotten. And us, sitting on the end of his bed . . . before we could even turn around, they were all tucked in, it is late for them, outside the sun is a frozen explosion in the ravaged emptiness of space . . .

Drag yourself out of the sleeping bag, get up. We flit after him. Watch him drink some water. Melted ice, extremely ancient water, trapped there since time immemorial, ever since two hydrogen atoms combined, *pop*, with an oxygen atom. The taste of a pure molecule, the pure taste of H_2O. Add to it the mineral salts prescribed by the medic, and it is even more disgusting, so they all get the shits, and the incinolettes have problems keeping up, so they blow a fuse and get jammed – Peter wouldn't do Jan Perse's job for the world. Anyway. He has the regular purr of the generator in his ears, like a huge, tame beast. Just remember to order more gaskets. The ones in the storeroom have been eaten through by the frost, like everything here, the plastic of the floorboards, the putty around the windows . . . Even the sheet metal is cracking, if such a thing is possible, and the books, and their skin . . . His dry lips. The lipstick she uses. Maybe he should use it too? Everything is collapsing and falling apart. During the day, you can hear the thaw at work, in relative terms. Things split open, separate, become disjointed. And, presumably, when the winter and the night fall again, they will start growing closer again, reaching out to each other, tightening, until they finally snap . . . And every year, whatever the weather, humans come back to get the boat afloat once more, and the building site, and the radio, to bodge it all up, and away we go again! The urinal. And, why not go for a stroll outside. Dry-suit. Boots. Gloves. Balaclava.

Glasses. And this exhausting daylight, the sun tattooed high in the sky . . .

Peter Tomson breathes, breathes in the crushed ice that passes for air, which seizes his lungs, anaesthetises his sore throat, and he counts automatically: one step, two steps. Three steps, and four and five, and up to twelve, *thud thud thud thud*, a song comes back to him . . . in the language of that land, that's it, something about the seasons, and renewal, windmills maybe? . . . his old nanny . . . or flights of birds coming back, images, that's it, a rhythm, a round, *la la la* . . .

Why not stay here, outside, in the light. Strips of mist, far off, below the sun, as if the snow was fading away from the effect of unknown rays; a blinding sky, with blue shadows amassed on the horizon . . . large herds on the plains . . . swarms of hallucinations . . . bells . . . a stable, the sea . . . You should be able to locate yourself just from the light. The globe, the one hundred and eighty arcs of longitude, multiplied by the ninety rings of latitude, and at each of these points capture the light: nowhere is it the same, migrating birds must perceive that. What Peter likes about the light here, at the Pole, is its nakedness. Just as it can be on occasion on the high seas, when all you can see is the horizon, when you are at a point between up and down, and you can sense the sphere. A hemisphere above, a hemisphere below, sky and sea, and snow here. There has been no ozone layer here for ages. Pete Tomson looks up instinctively at this absence, which burns even through his pure ultraviolet glasses. The sky is mauve – lie down in the snow and spin . . .

In the 1990s in Iceland, there were still fewer than forty trees, and they all had names. When heads of state came on official visits, a spade was thrust into their hands and

there we go, another tree. The George Bush tree. The
François Mitterrand tree. The Helmut Kohl tree. Pete
Tomson can remember that sensation, the lack of trees . . .
of having dreamt, lying on the ground . . . green shimmering in his eyes . . . yes, he once had that green shimmering
in his eyes, and in Iceland, like here, there is just the naked
sky above your head. Except that here, the sky really is
naked, it is a sky that has no stories, the sun falls straight
down on to a shadowless surface – lie beneath the trees
and dream, the leaves shimmering in your eyes – naked
space, naked sun and no stories, only the buzzing of the
generator, and perhaps a very soft sound of breathing . . .
and voices? . . . a whisper, sliding . . . a discreet *scratch*, as if
someone had detached the sky from the ground in one go,
and what will emerge from the gap? . . . Pete Tomson
shakes himself, half frozen. He notices the video room, he
passes by its door and we through the walls.

A scooter. She has a little helmet, which clearly does not
satisfy safety standards, and which lets her brown curls
blow free. Paris to her right, Paris to her left, opens out
behind her like the two flaps of a dress. Blue sky with little
white clouds, the passing mirrors of windows, pigeons *flap*
flap flap, trees and green buses and terraces – she is in a
sunny room, she speaks, *tipiti tapa tût*, in little stabs of
French, from the front of her mouth, beneath her lips,
enamel points and a clicking tongue, and those cracking
sounds, as if she was chewing nuts on the tips of her teeth,
it vibrates without rolling, it is nasal too, but only slightly,
a half measure, a touch of falsetto, the subtitles in Italian
just as incomprehensible – he knows the speeches by heart,
sound by sound, he chews through them *tipiti tapa* – someone, out of frame, answers the girl, the camera performs a

strange manoeuvre to locate the man who is replying, which gives Pete Tomson enough time to get ahead of it, fast forward mentally, reflections on a swinging window – and there she is again, white raincoat and extremely thin leather boots, it is raining, the scooter across gleaming tarmac, the slight shock when she takes her helmet off, the movement of her hair, her fingers brushing absent-mindedly through it, she orders a coffee at a bar, something is bothering her, rain dribbling down the windows, at the moment she leaves, he will hold the door open for her and offer her his umbrella, as one does in such countries, at the end of the walk they will dodge the puddles, laughing, *splish splash splosh* under her pretty boots, and drops will gather in the hollows of her jawbones, under her cheeks, here, pause . . .

The air rips open, *SCRATCH!* Pete Tomson presses stop, and we turn round as one ghost . . .

Edmée Blanco closes the strip of canvas behind her, flattening the Velcro with the palm of her hand . . .

And on the tray, she has brought: a tetrapak of milk, a dessert dish, a spoon and a pair of scissors, a packet of castor sugar and a spray can of whipped cream . . .

'Hello!' she says.

We say nothing. The Zurich Orchestra, whose plane crashed in the Andes in 1963, starts up a muted interlude.

"*Tipiti tapa tût?*" Pete Tomson would so like to be able to say as well.

She sits down one chair away from him (we quickly take the one in the middle, we scramble, pile up on top of one another, the pile tumbles over and we spin round while the Zurich Orchestra plays a tune for musical chairs – spiral, poltergeist, *wheeee!*).

69

'Please go on,' says Edmée, and Peter presses 'Play'.

Can you hear the sound of the telly, when you come in from outside?

Is she going to take off her anorak?

Seen from side on like that, from the corner of his eye, her profile is blue/green in the gleam of the television, with deep jutting shadows, and a black, hemispherical eye sunk into the triangle of her eyelid.

She undoes the Velcro of her shell boots, then she unlaces her shoes, undoes her gaiters.

With the tips of her toes, she pulls over another chair and puts her feet up on it.

Socks of white crocheted wool, immaculate, down-like, she wriggles her toes and even (her legs are free now that she has put down her tray) places her right foot on her left thigh and massages it (wherever did she get socks like that?).

(We knit away in Edmée's socks, we card, and wind, and spin, and roll ourselves up, thread by thread, purl by pearl.)

Vroom goes the scooter, *plip plop* goes the rain, the large yellow M of the Parisian metro passes by . . .

The rain is making charming reflections on Edmée's face, mirroring droplets, which roll down, as though she were sitting on the other side of the window, drinking her coffee with a far-away air, that perfect little Parisian air of don't-pay-me-any-attention . . .

And – wait – now she is cutting open the pack of milk with her scissors . . .

She takes out the cardboard box and goes at it with rapid snips of her blades, as though crushing almonds . . .

She fills her plate with lumps of milk, covers them with sugar and whipped cream, *whoosh!*, and without taking her eyes off the screen, eats her ice-cream so casually that all you can do is sit back agog.

A good downpour, that is what's needed, drops on your face, going for a walk, lingering, in the rain, in an inhabitable exterior, a good downpour – and puddles, mud, Iceland, the damp metal fences, the sheep and the taste of fog in your mouth, that sulphurous, steamy fog . . . and the metal slats under the wheels of the jeep, *ra-ta-ra-ta*, when they crossed the cattle grids . . . When he was six, his feet were still small enough to slip through, like animals' hooves, it scared him . . . but very soon, eight, nine years old, he could walk confidently, like an adult, no longer having to act the tightrope walker – the dogs leapt straight over, proud to go with him – and the rain fell on the countryside, which was like nothing else, large stretches of fluorescent moss, craters of orange sulphur, blue mud that bubbled and sheep eating lichen. Mr Gudmundsson was a cheese maker. Mr Gudmundsson's ancestor had already taken in refugees during the Second World War, and his great-grandson was keeping up the family tradition and the values of a neutral country. The cheese was brown and cubic, wrapped in cellophane. During meals, it was sliced into strips with a special cutter that looked like nothing else on earth.

You could hardly call it a country, a real country, a land. You could even wonder if you had not been dropped off somewhere else other than the Earth, on another planet, with creatures pretending to be sheep, and others playing at being dogs, schoolchildren and philanthropic shepherds, but which a simple change of viewpoint, of vision, would suddenly turn into something strange. Where he, Peter, would be the only little boy with warm blood and vertebrae. There was nothing left of his mother tongue, absolutely nothing of the language he had presumably spoken until the age of six, under a different name. Nothing, not a rhythm, not a sound, it was as if a switch had been thrown in his head. Apparently, this kind of amnesia is common among uprooted children; but then it is usually accompanied by a corresponding hypermnesia, the spectacular absorption of the host language, at the speed at which a sea sponge soaks up thirty times its weight in liquid in just a few seconds. Except that this time, that was not the case. Could it be that Peter was particularly bad at languages, or that Icelandic was a particularly tough nut to crack? But if you think of Basque, Estonian or Georgian, then surely that cannot be true. So Peter (who had been baptised thus because his original name was unpronounceable), little Peter was not very talkative from 1992 to 1997, when his parents reappeared, just like that, along with his nanny, Nana, but without his sister Clara, whose internationally pronounceable name had brought her no luck. But in any case, when it came to Clara, the nanny, his father and mother, Peter Tomson did not have the slightest idea who these people were.

So, when he was thirteen, Peter, or whatever his name was, left the Gudmundssons and moved in with his real parents and his old Nana in a prefabricated home loaned by the Icelandic government, in association with the UN refugee agency. And, for convenience's sake, the family decided to call itself Tomson, Tømson, or Tömson, as you wish. Tomson was a very common name, and it was also the brand of electrical appliances that equipped the prefabricated housing. When Peter left to study in Reykjavik, he was enrolled under the name Thomson and discovered, as if he had been able to put down his luggage at last, that he could find some sort of stability in his approximate English, spoken by half the planet. In any case, Peter was no longer the son of Tom, or of anyone else, and that suited him down to the ground.

He runs after the metro . . . In zero gravity, the doors are about to close, *cl-ack* . . .

On the platform, there is a . . . gypsy woman? A many-coloured scarf, shawl, skirts. Understands nothing she is telling him . . .

The lines of his hand? She is thirty with a child on her hip, she unfolds his fingers and her index tickles his palm with its hennaed nails – where has he seen that before?

He wants to tell her to get a move on, because the cops have appeared at the other end of the platform . . .

So, what did he say then? She puts the child down on the platform, they run off together . . .

'She's old enough to look after herself,' she says.

He feels completely reassured.

Up the high escalator steps four at a time, the mechanism is becoming increasingly erratic . . .

At each level, each concourse, he gazes around, three or four women – or men? – are now with him . . .

Along the broken-down escalators, people are living, who encourage them, removing obstacles from in front of them – cardboard boxes, parcels of books, brushwood, bundles of sticks . . .

On the following levels, the stairs narrow into dark, deserted bottlenecks. It is cold, the wind rises. When they emerge, they find themselves in a mountain meadow, along a pass, with clouds at hand's reach . . . a metallic smell in the wisps of fog . . . a sharp waft of oxygen . . . The grass has been flattened and is very pale, the snow must only just

73

have melted. It is still winter. Nothing to be seen further off. They go down a few steps. It is the evening. They are in a small coastal town, huge waves surge up, frothing against the ancient harbour walls. He finds his house again. He is now alone. He recognises his bed in the half-light, the unmade sheets, still warm, and he lies down.

But something nags at him. It is a pain having to stay awake, it is a pain in the head, crossing your brain, not to let yourself slip under . . . Ringing . . . insistently . . .

What the hell is he doing here? Half off his chair. Edmée. The generator, that repetitive *ouiiii*, like the wailing of an abandoned new-born babe . . . They were watching the film, the only film worth watching that he has found here, the Parisian girl on her scooter . . . and she was eating frozen milk. He must have looked stupid, asleep on his chair. And he lives in a universe where the slightest step outside means wrapping yourself up, doing up your dry-suit, pulling on your boots . . . quick . . .

The slap from the sun makes Peter stagger. Tears fill his eyes at once. Glasses . . .

He closes his eyes and the dream starts up again, the bed, the sheets . . . the coastal town and the harbour wall, that's it . . . the relaxation of a dream, yellow cut stone, encrusted with shells and the grassy mountain pass and that many-coloured fabric – in Aberdeen? Were there gypsy women when he worked in Aberdeen?

What's the time? Just twenty seconds since the alarm started up . . . a sensation of having run along kilometres of harbour wall . . .

Anyway, there is no continuity from one dream to the next. The feeling of having borrowed dreams here and there, when passing through. From one person or another, one me here, another me there. Here, everyone dreams, a lot, so much that they talk about it over breakfast. But not her, unless it is insignificant, trivial things, like seeing the sea, seeing trees or the rain, or animals. She is right, there is nothing more obscene than dreams, people just dream of what they do not have, that's all. Nothing to say. Sheets, a room of your own. Meadows, seasons, a truly desert-like desert.

It is a gasket that has gone, a gasket as wide as a ribbon, below the storage tank. One has blown here, but any of the other ones could just as well have blown also. When removed from its channel, it rips like paper, fissures and tiny bubbles. (The effects of the cold – unceasing amazement.)

Bodge it up with aluminium tape, that should hold until he can pinch a gasket from one of the Caterpillars, or God knows where. Phone the coast, get them to fly some gaskets over. The alarm stops. *Phew*. The engine turns. It is nice and warm here, why not go back to sleep.

It is a place for doing nothing, what he suspects about her is that she is like him: here to do nothing. Fed and watered, no questions to churn over. The incredible distance. Work as justification. Him with his generator, her with her radio. You might just as well stay where the real problem is. And so try and think of nothing, let the season go by, wait for the fat cheque, and that's it. Start again the following year. Most of them live like that. With no place of their own on the planet, living in hotels until it starts again, choosing the Côte d'Azur or a little yacht in the Caribbean . . . Pendulum return trips between the Pole and the rest of the world. And, to appear normal, they say they are from somewhere, their home towns are written up on the post in front of the base, along with the distance in kilometres: Firenze, 16,500 km; Tallinn, 18,200 km; Oslo, 18,500 km. Exaggerating cultural tics, hamming up accents, getting into nationalist frenzies about next to nothing, ha ha! In the eye of the storm, by the signpost. She is apparently French, or Canadian, or so he has heard . . . She lives in Texas, in Houston? NASA. Rockets.

They are incredibly far from Iceland here. They are incredibly far from anywhere, from any point of origin, unless you consider the Pole to be the centre of somewhere. The centre of nothingness, then. Apart from Mars, you cannot get any further away. Icelanders say that they are born with an elastic band on their backs, always eager to leave their lump of lava, but always coming back. Nostalgia for Iceland is an emotion that Peter was not expecting. But they are so isolated here, that you could feel nostalgic about anywhere, anywhere that was warm and alive. This post stuck up in front of the living quarters, with its place names and distances . . . Once more the idea inches its way – piccolo, slowly does it – into Peter's mind. How about cutting out some cardboard? Write on it: Húsavík? Calculate the number of kilometres? Find some wire and climb up the post? Every time he goes by this post, which is ten times a day, the idea arises then vanishes, without Peter being personally involved in this brief dispute, his brain argues away on its own, as his body moves on, the generator to be repaired, the generator has been repaired, see a film, film seen, dinner, digestion, avoid the others, others avoided for thirty seconds . . . As the cold permits, Peter paces up and down, twenty steps, the well-beaten track outside the living quarters. He sees a car go by, and far in the distance, a traffic jam. The sound of horns – or is it bells? A ringing in his ears. The silence is so deep you can hear your layers rustle. The wind in the poplars – a suburb of Aberdeen, three years with British Petroleum. Their incomprehensible English. Rain on your face. Rain on the windows. And that incomprehensible Scots girl. The smell of the refinery. What time is it? Breakfast.

One day, he will take a snow scooter and go to the South Pole, fifteen kilometres away. It will make a good excursion. And to the geographical South Pole, the one reached by Scott and Amundsen, not the other, magnetic one, which shifts about with the waves. Maybe even he will sense something, waves, or a centre? Where the curves and currents converge? He will treat himself to that much. In such a silence, he will still be able to hear the alarm. The only snag is that you have to go in twos, the rules do not allow anyone to go on their own. Which only goes to show that he was quite wrong in coming here, where solitude is the rarest of luxuries. Physical solitude, that is, because here they really are alone, if you let yourself slide down the slope of nothingness. Seventy-five kilos of living flesh, against a continent of white nothingness. One metre eighty tall above kilometres of snow as old and ignorant as water is old and ignorant.

Adopt his parents' dream, the desert, isolation. Cultivate his snow garden, grow roses, sculpt lava, erect stone totems. He knows all about that. Thought he had escaped. Letting the world slip by him like a cloud. And then, what had they told him? Nana's voice, not his parents of course: his sister Clara – not a single memory of her – and what war can do to girls. Thought they were rich enough to let it blow over. He was already safe and in Iceland. Why didn't they send them together? Their progeny. Why him and not her, why her and not him, and so on? And what exactly happened, what happened *exactly* – no idea. He witnessed nothing.

Survived nothing. In the middle of nothing. What did he think he would find in this place?

The blue, extremely blue sky, with this soft wind from nowhere and the turbine . . . *chip* . . . *chip* . . . and the generator . . . *zoooom*. *Dong* from the hallucinatory bells. He was the one who wanted to come here. Or rather: who answered the ad, who let himself be taken out here. Shackleton's advertisement in *The Times* in 1906: '*Men wanted for hazardous journey. Low wages, bitter cold, long hours of complete darkness. Safe return doubtful. Honour and recognition in event of success.*' Everyone has a story, and that's all there is to it. To be in charge of a stupid heating system, fed, lodged, watered. Get up, go to bed. The round sun and the ice. Stop zigzagging around now, pushing your ball along like a circus bear. The winds unfurl in wider and wider circles around the Pole. As they spiral out along the coast, then over the open sea, they speed up, into the screaming sixties, the furious fifties and the roaring forties . . . here there is the turbine, *chip chip*.

That Canadian, that Frenchie, that girl, *Edmée*. She only has ten or fifteen metres to do between the kitchen and her booth, but she is still completely dressed up. She waves to him. He nods his head. In her gloves, she is carrying a steaming tray, her tea will be ice cold by the time she arrives, but he understands her: she is now shutting herself up alone more and more often in her little radio booth. It is almost as if she is living there now. He pictures the place, full of crumbs, empty packs of milk, spoons pinched from the kitchen, biscuits and tea bags. Hairbrush, and books . . . maybe a framed photo? She does not have any children, so far as he knows. An earth, a mouse's nest.

We play at being mice around Pete Tomson. We scamper. We nibble. But the girls among us stop the game – *shush!*

Someone is playing in silence next to Peter. Cutting out cardboard shapes, perhaps from a magazine. Snipping out naked bodies, and two-dimensional clothes. Positioning the clothes over the bodies thanks to judiciously placed tabs. This memory, if it is one, is very far from the surface of Peter's mind. Nearer to the centre, there where nothing moves and nothing arrives; there where nothing circulates, neither the fossilised nursery rhymes, nor the taste of milk, frozen for ever; where the wind will never slam a door shut, or bring fresh air. Only we can enter here. In the cellar. Peter shakes his head and fidgets. We pull back. Echoes. The little girl stops moving her scissors.

Go back to bed for an hour or two? A film, now the room is free? Or make some hot tea in the kitchen? Start the day – in bed or up, what does it matter when it comes to watching over the generator? The memory, if it is one, has become so slight that even we ghosts are having problems making out the tiny sound of the scissors and of the cardboard being folded over. No images, if there ever were any. Maybe it was a dream memory. One of those floating memories that go from mind to mind. That drift about the world and condense here, when the wind falls. They form tiny puddles and ooze into invisible cracks, down to the lakes. Sooner or later, he is going to have to call up his mother. Or Mr Gudmundsson and Mrs Gudmundsdottir, who are so proud of having turned him into a real Viking, of the breed that crosses the seas to conquer the Pole and its hardships. Whatever. That, too, can wait.

Everyone wanted to phone. It was an evening ritual, after the routine messages, the weather forecast and the despatches. There was about an hour's satellite time left, and Edmée – one of the perks of the job – had already called Samuel. Three in the afternoon in Houston. Sam was at work, which was not very convenient, often he could not really talk because he had a glass office; mostly, he turned off the 3-D projectors, which made their communication a touch old-fashioned. He whispered, in shirtsleeves despite the air conditioning, leaning forward to make their conversation as private as possible. As he could not see her, his eyes wandered over his keyboard, his plant, or his block of Post-Its. Pensive and touching, isolated in his transparent office and, at the same time, strangely given over to her. His colleagues had already talked enough about his wife's polar attraction for her sudden appearance in her orange dry-suit, her nose burnt by the frost, in front of a military radio, not to seem untoward.

Then Edmée went to the living quarters to tell them it was time – everyone had their allotted turn – and to hand out the international dispatches: politics, wars, trade, sometimes scientific news, or else amusing anecdotes. She returned to her booth with the first in line. Since she could not go to Mars, it was here that she had come for a real change; and now she was beginning to enjoy watching these wives and children appear, with babies pointing at their fathers, and older ones asking for a zoom on his fluorescent boots or a glance beneath the Velcro on the window. Were there any bears around? Had they thawed out any extra-terrestrials? Some of the fathers shot footage during the day, and Edmée occasionally let them broadcast a couple of minutes of it as a favour, showing a successful drill core, or the five suns, or huge plates of pasta and don't we eat well here. But there was rarely enough satellite time, so the fathers told it as best they could.

It was evening in Tallinn, with decorated pine cones in the windows – Christmas – a red light in a cosy kitchen and a blonde woman. It was morning in Vladivostok, a sturdy woman in the uniform of a maritime customs officer – in the port: you could hear the gulls, you could see a stretch of grey water and some concrete slabs at her feet. It was sleeting. The 3-D motor was struggling a bit and white flashes were zigzagging across the booth, how much depth to give to a snowflake? There were also old women, who stood too close; dogs; cats; hospital sheets; newly delivered dishwashers; children's drawings; pullovers being knitted and growing larger. Edmée sometimes wanted these women to move about, to reveal their surroundings, but her business was to remain as discreet as possible. They kissed and she looked aside in the five square metres of her canvas booth. Sometimes they said hello to her, asked after her, she bent down to smile straight into the screen, into a Spanish or Danish living room. Most of the time, they ignored her, which suited her just fine.

Sometimes the distance, the separation, got to her colleagues – when the image went out, Edmée then had to take a few seconds of satellite time to cheer them up a bit, to tell them that she had a husband, too, and that six months in the life of a couple, what did that really come down to? The Imp always tried to cadge a few extra seconds, he made her laugh to gain some time, but as soon as the hologram of his wife lit up the booth – a shifting, blue, Parisian light – all that was left for Edmée was to stick her boots under her chair so that the camera would catch as little of her as possible. The Imp was now on the other side of the world. His face faded. His orange dry-suit stayed sitting on his chair like an empty shell, and he was in his kitchen with his wife, or he was bouncing his son on his lap, or he was slipping between the sheets of the conjugal bed, yes, she had even placed a camera there. And the French they spoke together was a language Edmée had never heard before, made up of bird calls, mimicry and melodies, grimaces, harmonicas and flutes, with sometimes the *crash bang* of a brass band. His wife burst out laughing, or into tears, chatted volubly, and the Imp did likewise but at different times. They drew nearer, touching and embracing and trilling and singing and flapping and dancing extraordinary steps. Sometimes, their son joined in the dance, crawling between them, so quickly that his little feet and hands were often lost from the image. They spun themselves into a sphere from which Edmée felt herself hurtling away at an increasingly alarming speed. And no matter how much she fiddled with the controls, or pretended to adjust the image, or watched out for an emergency call which would have forced her to interrupt, she was all ears for that incredible language.

The man who emerged from these sessions was no longer recognisable. His slack face was in pieces, apparently seen head on and in profile at the same time. He tried to pull his balaclava over it. Sometimes, she left them alone, him and her, and took refuge in the living quarters despite the unpleasantness of such round trips in the cold. There was something abnormal, something she could not bear between that man and that woman. When she returned to the booth, the Imp's chair had been pulled over to where the hologram had formed; and she pictured him, arms round his wife, lips open, body tense, mouth empty, and she winced just like when you bite into a cold ice-cream.

Then came Jan Perse, who had a number of women and called each of them in turn; Claudio and his family in Florence; the Queen Mum's man on an oil rig; and Dimitri, the Russian. She enjoyed the company of Dimitri and of his sturdy other half in her customs officer's uniform. The thaw had set in at Vladivostok. The thaw and dawn. Piles of black snow were melting, drop by drop, on to the concrete. In the puddles, there were cigarette butts, matches, gravel, a flyer folded in four, an apple core and dark, floating matter. A translucent film, like paraffin, made the water iridescent. When the connection was established, his wife was lighting a cigarette – the flame was what you saw first – and Dimitri leant forwards, his elbows on his knees, squinting with a pained expression. The uniform's very austerity meant that it came up on the screen all at once, followed by the lighter areas of the face and hands, and her expression, the sky, and the concrete slabs and puddles, close and clear, which so absorbed Edmée. When the woman's boots paddled in them, the pale film broke up into jagged-edged blotches. The air in the booth grew heavier as the men took their turns, it got hotter and hotter, from time to time Edmée lifted up a few centimetres of Velcro to take a breath of chill air. The two Russians unrolled the waves of their language, and Edmée was agreeably lost and lulled by their syllables. These two never had much to say to each other, maybe it was not the right time of day. Or else, Russian is such a wonderfully compact language that it expresses a great deal with a minimum of gushing. *Matriochka spassiba samovar Tolstoi*, was all Edmée knew how to say in Russian. And *liub* something or other, a palatalised sound, the vague recollection of how to say *I love you* (when little, that doll which said *I love you* in twenty-five languages).

The cigarette shortened in odourless wisps. The conversation emptied itself out calmly, water in the mouth and a whistling of air, the sounds *u* and *r*, minor collapses and unexpected rises. Dimitri's hands trembled and his fore-head was still pained, maybe it was not being able to smoke, many smokers find it hard to abstain on the phone. The smoke drifted around his partner, but stopped dead at the frame which also cut through the sky and the concrete, the sky being just a little darker in the corners, and the concrete more sombre, because of the echo. Edmée worked hard at finding the best setting, but it was the face that mattered most; when everything was stable, she went back to the puddles. The woman was soon going to drop her cigarette and crush it with her heel, and the conversation would be over. She would walk out of the frame while Dimitri was standing up; then he would head for the dormitory, and her to the end of the quay, or so she supposed. Seagull cries. Enter into the hologram and follow those heavy boots, paddling in the puddles, *splash*. Stare at the sea. Watch birds fly past. Remember sparrows, blackbirds. Buy bread and go home past the gardens. If we were just made of memories, we would be able to feel the bread melting beneath our teeth and hear the birds, breathe in the flowers and wind, with Edmée Blanco.

Officially, Edmée's shift finished at 2300 local time; an arbitrary moment, given that any rotating time could have fitted in with the movement of this sun. There was often a little satellite contact remaining before the Pole left the link-up zone. The satellite was Indian, and the only one to navigate so far down, and all the holophone lines ran through New Delhi. Once, a crossed connection put Edmée in touch with someone up there, and they had jokingly exchanged news of the weather. 'It is cold and very very far away,' Edmée said to describe the place where she was calling from, and the man at the other end of the line replied: 'Like Mars.' No one knows where Antarctica is.

Everyone is obsessed with Mars, because the heroes are about to set foot there. Sam was not working on the project directly, but of course he spoke about it. Edmée often managed to hook up with Houston again before disconnection time. It was a poor-quality moment, Sam had a double, his head drifted several centimetres from his body. The important point was that he was able to project her, though she must be just as disjointed, because the office was now empty, and so they had to make the most of it. It was a pain not being able to see each other discreetly at home, in the morning or the evening. But local time had been determined according to specific criteria: to allow connection at a reasonable hour of the day with the coast, Europe, North America and Australia. This resulted in a time that was a compromise, neither fish nor fowl, so as to satisfy everyone. So, for six months, she would see Samuel in a suit and tie – except at weekends, of course, but weekends were a hassle, everyone wanted to call, especially those with children who went to school, otherwise . . .

She fixed herself up a bit, retied her ponytail, and smiled. The link-up started. Describe the five suns in a few minutes; the naked snow; the endless day; the fact that often they were actually too hot rather than too cold; how awkward hygiene was, the tiny dribble of water in the showers and the stink of the incinolettes; the alarm of the generator, especially at night, which made her heart leap (and she thought of the Headcase, who had to get dressed at full speed and go out into the bright sunlight at two in the morning); the landscape around the aerial; the wind turbine as slow as the sun. Yes, you could say it was beautiful, but it was no bundle of laughs. Yes, she was pleased with her trip. No, she wasn't bored. It was doing her good to work a bit again, that's right, it was doing her good. Was it weird being the only woman among so many men?

(We rustled in, *flttfltt*, between Sam and Edmée.)

No, she didn't think so.

The glaciologists were drilling, they had now reached three thousand metres, deeper than the Americans, they hoped to reach the lake in two weeks' time. As for the workmen, they were expected any day now. There would be more of a crush, and twice as much work for her as an operator, but it would be good to see progress being made on the site.

The lake?

The lake in the depths, the lake between the bedrock and the ice, the lake beneath their feet, far away, liquid, primal water . . .

She could hear the humming of the air conditioning in Sam's office, which made the hum of the generator audible too. Usually they only paid attention to it when it stopped. Sam looked at her, or did not look at her, depending on whether he could bring up her image or not. As she was now alone, alone with Sam, she could wear only a tee-shirt and fan herself with her gloves. A tiny draught passed through the loose Velcro and hit her in the nape of the neck like an icy guillotine. Sam looked at her, with the same pained squint as Dimitri, the same question mark between his eyebrows: her, with her orange dry-suit rolled down over her hips, her breasts, sweat stains under her armpits at minus forty degrees C and her radio apparatus bodged up with sticking tape; or else he looked at his keyboard, his hands, the transparent air in front of him. And – depending on whether his gaze stopped half-way from hers (as, in a mirror, vision meets itself at an equal distance

86

between pupil and reflection), midway above the curve of the planet, with a minuscule delay between the sound of their breathing and the movement of their chests; or whether his gaze became lost in the folds of the air and so projected shapes, faces, memories – she told him, or did not, that she missed him.

Little girls danced in a circle and were gone. Bordeaux and the Gironde and Vancouver and Georgian Bay were gone. The fountain on the estate and the tricycles and the swing were gone. Behind Samuel, through the glass partitions of his office, she could make out the perpetual blue halo in the Houston sky. She put her face to the image (especially if he could not see her) and tried to get a better look at the trees and large park beneath NASA's windows. The photograms quivered, the green blotch of the park wobbled, lawns came in flashes. On entering the image, its objects broke apart, everything became green, yellow, blue, and Sam's three dimensions warped, his mouth slithered downwards, his arms drooped along his sides like creepers. Trying to touch each other was ridiculous, or to dance together, like the Imp tried to do with his wife. Very young children ran towards their hologrammed parents and crossed straight through the room, *whoosh*. She sat down again. The Earth shifted, the Pole/satellite angle opened until it split. Samuel flashed and was then sliced in half through his solar plexus. The Pole left the link-up zone and Edmée imagined it leaving the planet. More and more lines blew, the connections broke, Sam's hands fell from his arms and formed independent, hazy spheres. The top of his head was scalped, soon his mouth vanished, nothing was left of his office; and his voice slowed down, a record from her childhood played at the wrong speed; he became incomprehensible, she waved goodbye to him and *flop!* the booth was empty.

Pete Tomson leans idly over the eyepiece in the drill. He cannot see anything, of course, because human vision is incapable of dealing with a three-kilometre-long tube, no wider than two hands forming a circle. For this reason, a 3-D screen provides a synthetic image of the hole, in particular showing the properties of its sides, given that it will soon be used to extract water from the lakes, *fingers crossed*. As they are now nearing their objective, they have had to abandon the standard drill, rotors and lubricants. It is out of the question to pollute the water with glycol, so they are now descending with a high-tech melt and rinse drill-head, which melts the ice at the end of a cable. Peter sometimes gets flashes of panic when he remembers that everything around here – everything that bangs and clatters, the pulley motors, reels and drill-head – works off the generator. The vibration of the machinery, the serious faces of the glaciologists bending over their screens – over this hole – this is more than just the usual water from a tap. The drill cores are filed away in a freezer according to the age of the ice: under a thousand years, under two thousand years, and so on . . . as they go down, they run into the Romans, the Cro-Magnons, Lucy, then presumably no one, the dinosaurs, algae, amoebae, then really no one, gases, lava, the unimaginable, matter, nothing you can get a grip on . . .

Peter Tomson watches the drill cores come up. They call him over when they have a new one, because they know he is interested, they have a little celebration with defrosted champagne and ultra-dry crackers. Soon, the pressure at the bottom of the hole will be so great that it will have to be kept closed all the time, by adjusting the melt and rinse head so that the ice freezes again instantly behind it, thus forming a perfect seal. Otherwise, as soon as the drill touches the lake, the water will burst out with such force that the entire base will be washed away (a geyser, thinks the Icelandic part of Pete Tomson). In the end, he is not the only one to have the fate of the base in his hands. With his drill and his lake, the mild-mannered Imp could wipe them all off the map, supposing they were on anyone's map. Anyway: Pete Tomson watches the ice come up, and we sigh, it reminds us of the days when there was nothing, when there were not even days . . . And these long tubes of raw, blue, deep-frozen time which the glaciologists are extracting, millimetre by millimetre, carefully clutched in their gloves, make Peter philosophical. There is a hush. Everyone realises that they do not even occupy a micron's length of all this, and they chew their metaphysics between their upper and lower molars. What comes back to Pete Tomson are all the flotsam and jetsam he has been burdened with over the years, the bracelets, rings, medallions, photos, locks of hair, and then there is his father's watch and his mother's solitaire, and his sister's gold chain – when being thrown overboard, little Peter had been given plenty of ballast (like the story he used to read in his teens, about cosmonauts being ejected from their capsule with just one hour's reserve of oxygen), and twenty-five years later he is leaning over this hole – scaffolding, hoists, conveyor belt, you cannot see the hole at all, it is absolutely nothing like he had imagined – and saying to himself that there would be no deeper, colder, more secret place to get rid of all that junk.

What kept him on the Earth, apart from the activity of his cells? Where was his rigging, his cables and anchor? What surroundings could he be placed in? He never came to call. Edmée observed him during meals, the Headcase, the Yogi, Peter. He did not laugh when Jan Perse mimed a serenade on his knees in front of her, and finished by yelling EDMEE, OH HEDMEE!! while rolling on the ground. But all you could do was laugh. If bombs went off around him, then he would probably just dust himself off with a bored look. 'The Headcase' was the nickname that stuck to him most firmly, like wreaths of debris in branches after a flood. Then there was the way he ignored her, Edmée; this was more than a mere lapse of taste, it was a professional foul, he could end up wrecking the atmosphere, and bursting the well-oiled hinges of their isolation. The regulations concerning Edmée might be tacit, but they were as clear as those dealing with a major breakdown, evacuation or a magnetic storm.

The way he stared elsewhere, into space, like everyone – could his loves, his desires be seen there? Or memories? Crimes? Was it just his country? His passport was Icelandic, but that didn't fit. What backdrop would appear in the booth, if ever he showed up there? An Indian goddess with several pairs of arms? A souk? A samovar? Orange or olive trees? An empty phone box? Or one of those crowded phone shops, its floor covered with cigarette butts and its walls with posters advertising holosex? It was almost easier to picture him being bombed, to place him in a disaster area, in one of those regional conflicts that are so seldom televised. Maybe that was his natural environment, his biotope. Ruins, a catastrophe, that sort of anonymity. Things fell apart before Edmée's eyes, smoking, spilling over, during those long conversations between Claudio and his Claudia, between the Queen Mum and his king.

What about knocking his glasses off his nose? Or else taking them off gently? She would reveal his closed eyelids, with his eyes rolling beneath them, like a dreaming cat. He would look at her and smile silently, that's what, he would stand up and invite her to join him, his hand held out. Waltz. Between the card players and the vodka lovers. Waltz. Music, music rising up from the pipe organs of ice, blowing through the crevasses, note by note through the drill cores, *toot toot*. With us dancing around Edmée and Peter, dancing and yelling 'Encore!' while stretching our bodies from limbo and whispering sweet nothings in their ears.

One of the only things the Douglastown estate had in common with the White Project base was the rainbow prism that formed above the sun. Through the spray of the sprinklers on the lawns of the estate, the Douglastown sun anticipated the colours of the Pole. The unceasing sprinklers, the rainbows of municipal water, were what Edmée saw from her window when she woke up: house-lawn-house-lawn. The fluffy line of trees in the park. The square basin of the fountain. A few swimming pools in the wealthiest road. Further off, the skyscrapers of Houston. And further off still, to the South, what remained of the old mangrove, a dark green line and sea mists. Crocodiles. When Edmée went down into the kitchen to make tea and tidy away the breakfast things, she could now see the play area, which was still empty at that time of day, and a section of the cycle path that spiralled between all the houses on the estate. The swing and the fountain were precisely at the centre of the whole thing, and Edmée Blanco liked to think that, seen from a satellite, her geographical position in the estate's architecture was a central one, too. For the same price, Edmée would have preferred to live down-town, in one of the skyscrapers, but there were no real shops there, and in the evenings it was not safe to go out, and Samuel had been a child in New Jersey at the time of 9/11, so nothing would make him live in a building of over three storeys. There was still something European about Edmée Blanco, about her way of life, her relation-ship with space, with America, that was part of her charm, but which, as she herself admitted, sometimes led her to complicate the simplest things. For example, she was less afraid of going downtown at night, or even of leaving for the South Pole – since no one had managed to get that idea out of her head – than of imagining herself growing old in Douglastown. Was it the similarity between all the houses? Those quiet afternoons? After the Higgins tragedy, she should have attended the psycho-logical debriefing sessions – but there, too, she had behaved eccentrically.

One day, she opened the front door to an itinerant sales-man. It was morning, not long before Imelda Higgins killed her children. From the upstairs bedroom window, Edmée had seen him coming from afar. No one opened their doors, of course. He was on foot and carrying a large portfolio of drawings. He rang the doorbells of the Falcones, the Stuarts and the Higginses, and it had to be Edmée who answered. In fact, they were not drawings, but aerial shots of the estate. The streets were all numbered and easy to find. Oddly enough, Edmée was not interested in her own house – photographed in the morning, with Sam's car still in the drive and the duvet being aired on the windowsill. No, instead Edmée Blanco chose an overview of the entire estate, taken from slightly higher up, with the blue square of the fountain, the play area, the first row of houses (including hers, with the tiny patch of the duvet), the second row, and the third and so on, as far as the sixth, the snail trail of the cycle path, the cross of the four access roads, and the beginning of the intersection with the free-way going to Houston. A kind of logo for a sect of sun worshippers, or else a target. The Buick convertible is at the Stuarts' house, in row three. The bikes and tricycles are in the Higginses' drive, row two. No one is out and about yet, everything is gleaming and empty, it is a lovely day, the lawns are sparkling, the arc of the sprinklers can even be seen in places, indigo, blue, green, yellow, orange and red. You can imagine Edmée and Samuel still at home, if you took off their roof, they would be minuscule, with her reading in her dressing-gown on the unmade bed, and him eating eggs in the kitchen. It is a pleasant, fresh moment, full of promise. Anyway, Edmée paid cash for the photo, found a frame at Hallmark and put it on top of the televi-sion in the living room. It was one of Edmée Blanco's little eccentricities: a direct path led from that photo to the South Pole.

We ghosts liked curling up around it, too. We could pic-ture it as the centre of something, Edmée Blanco's town centre. It was not such a bad place to live, it was not like living in the sixth row, for instance, or worse, as far out as the intersection. Here, she had a view of the fountain, which was a little bit, a tiny little bit, like having the sea; a chance to breathe. Here, she could daydream at her win-dow, watch the play area and pass the time with the to-ing and fro-ing of bikes. Because, in any case, since the Big Bang, since the beginning of the beginning, we were all being chased away farther and farther out by the centrifu-gal force of the explosion; because, in any case, Samuel and NASA alongside him had confirmed the fact: the centre had been lost. The kernel, the zero point, the heart of hearts had – *pfut!* – been pulverised.

It vanishes like a puddle evaporating, edges shrinking, absorbed by the whiteness . . . Then it comes back, a line that thickens, rising above the horizon and apparently labouring under the effort . . . one moment near, the next moment far . . . beneath it, the transparent sky quivers . . . Edmée's eyes weep. Here, eyes can see nothing, and the creaking sound in her ears is coming from the bottom of the sea. Silence brings forth ghosts and mirages give them form. A railway station bell, suddenly, announces an abstract time . . . a message is being broadcast – a summons? You can never hear anything in stations, what with crowds, suitcases on wheels, high metal girders, Europe, and that smell of grey platforms . . . *How far I am*, Edmée's mental language becomes indeterminate. She scrapes the satellite dish, *scratch scratch* . . . The fight against frost . . . When she looks up, she can make out the vehicles of the convoy, small objects veiled with a red optical vibration, as if this extremely rare arrival of something should be signalled again and again . . . Edmée calls out 'Hey-o' unconvincingly, if the role of watcher has fallen to her, she does not feel particularly excited about it. What is the protocol? It's the workmen they have been expecting. There will be some action on the building site. New conversations. A few days ago, Edmée would have felt a breath of fresh air inside her – go announce the news – a little hooray in her chest, as she sweats and pants along the path to the living quarters. Claudio picks up his binoculars. They are still several hours' drive away. Everything moves so slowly here . . . daybreak, nightfall, travellers . . . There is time to defrost the champagne and the crackers.

Should they warn the heating engineer, so he can turn up the boiler and be prepared for twice as many people? Claudio will deal with it. He's the boss.

To kill time, he watches the little French film again. But it no longer entertains him as it did. What he looks at now is, in fact, the way the actress kisses. Not that he thinks French girls kiss in a particular way. But you do say 'French kiss' in English. How old is this film? It doesn't say on the box. A 2-D movie. Ten or fifteen years probably. To judge by the dresses they wear. And the lipstick. While watching the actress in action, he remembers how some women – among the wearers of lipstick – apply it sideways, one swipe above, one below; others have a more direct, head-on approach so that the initially bevelled tip becomes round; others still purse their lips while sliding the lipstick between, thus sharpening it on both sides into a point – his mother used to do that. Her lipsticks, left all over the place, in the bathroom, car, settee in the living room . . . and in her studio . . . Peter winds the memory back into its little tube. No desire at all to think about his mother. He waits. He daydreams. There is never anything about France, the Imp complained one evening when the dispatches arrived. 'Why, did they invent a new sauce?' Edmée laughed with the jokers, looking as French as he does Icelandic.

The covering of weather spreads out. The covering of pale weather parked above Antarctica. An anticyclone of motionlessness; yet, the season is moving on, the sun is beginning to go down, the evening chill is more bitter, and the yellow rays are in line with their eyes. Mid-season. Peter browses Scott's diary. On that same date, 19 January, the devastated return from the Pole: 'Why is it that the tracks left by our sledge, which date from a mere three days, have partly been effaced, while those left by the Norwegians, which go back one month, are still visible?' Peter Tomson's preoccupations are quite different from those of Robert Falcon Scott, one century earlier; but it's not hard to imagine that the same vortex of dead time unravels here every year (we rush in); that blatant hollows are formed in the progression of time (we rush in); and that only winners like Amundsen manage to extricate themselves from them, whipping onwards their dogs and their hours.

Calm. We slip on light dresses, silk dressing-gowns and naked flesh. We offer up Edmée: Edmée here, Edmée over there. Peter chases us away. She is here, she is over there. This thought – these pronouns, verb and adverbs, whichever the language they are expressed in – makes him feel extraordinarily restful. Rest slides down his eyelids, his shoulders, his spinal cord. It feels as if a broad smile is turning up the edges of his diaphragm, raising his solar plexus and widening his ribcage. Pause. Nothing.

Through the canvas, a sinister gleam from the zenith. He lifts up the Velcro. A large, iced-white sun. No one between the buildings, just the glitters of this visible wind. The frost tumbles down in myriad forms, light, quick . . . A ravenous, multiple entity, everywhere . . . Six months away from it all had seemed to be synonymous with a degree of rest, and rest with a degree of happiness. The rest and happiness that his parents – or so he thinks – pursued relentlessly and unsuccessfully in other latitudes, in their garden and expensive villa, before the bombs which were falling not very far away, less and less far away, finally fell on them too. We draw near once more. Bombs and so on. He would so like not to think about all that now, right now. He has just been touched by another form of rest, but it has already changed its form again. No point insisting.

He puts on a film at random. It is a typical skinflick, a 3-D coloured red mostly, a prick in a cunt and *whish* and *whoosh*. There would be material for a film here, with the boredom and isolation, a base cut off and a ropey script, *The Operator gets Gangbanged* – he chases the idea away. We set our mirrors at a different angle in the light. The last time he saw his mother, she was casting totems on the slopes of a volcano; channelling the lava into cast-iron containers to solidify later in the air of the glaciers; and then she stood up her creatures among the natural forms. Elves, trolls, outlaws, witches. Forms at the foot of volcanoes in Iceland, *your mother is a brilliant artist*. He chases away the idea, the thing. Empty yourself. Yoga. With the alarm of the generator as random punctuation. He is used to that. The *ouiii ouiii* of a new-born baby's cries. Or the audible hyphens on an engaged telephone line; not even an adrenalin rush any more. He entertains himself by breaking his own records, as though on a Formula 1 circuit: three minutes for patching up a gasket; six minutes for filtering the oil; four minutes for washing the tank; two minutes for scraping clean a sparkplug – he has got the breakdowns under control. A good training for staying calm, for feeling time slow down and beat again at the same rhythm as his arteries – but now, he is waiting. The sun hangs from the top of the sky like a clock. With him on the edge of its face.

It never snows. The weather forecasts mention blizzards three hundred kilometres away; but here – nothing. Meteorologically, it is the most static place on the planet. The central point, the eye of the needle. The Pole. That this crossroad of geographical lines should be so like a periphery, that kilometre zero should be so deserted, appeals to Edmée's idea of world order. An epicentre that can be detected by its utter silence. Apparently, Siberian winters are as cold as Antarctic summers, but damp, very damp, while here the dry air is crisp. So damp that a heavy mist rises from the snow, a cotton-wool mist which splits apart as humans enter it, then lingers there . . . Hours later, you can see that an upright creature has passed this way, because the shape of a walking man floats there hollowly, a pale channel . . . Here, there is the white light that some-times engulfs the entire sky, right down to the ground, which it shrouds. And the emptiness is so intense, that anything which enters it leaves a trace, something of it remains in space: in the silence, in the whiteness, nothing-ness becomes peopled, too. Edmée knows that.

Stardust falls everywhere across the planet, as Ukla the astrophysicist explains to Edmée. He, too, wanted some tea. And Peter squirmed in front of his cup, before putting on his shoes, shell boots and hood and saying: 'I need to make a phone call this evening.' Even though no one asked him anything, he went on (inner mittens, mittens, gloves): 'It's urgent, it's for the generator.' 'Come along first, then,' Edmée says, and regrets it at once: 'Come along last,' that's what she should have said. When the others are asleep. The idea lingers there, floating . . . floating and lingering, when he has already gone into the cold, pre-sumably to the video room. *Stardust falls everywhere across the planet.* 'Eh?' says Edmée. 'Oh yes,' says Ukla. (He arrived with the workmen, he is still suffering from the altitude and breathing with difficulty.) 'On the pavements of cities, at the bottom of the ocean, among the grasses of the savannah, but to collect it, there is no other place on the planet that is so clean and so unpolluted. They've even given me a snow scooter so I can get away from the smoke of the incinolettes.' 'Eh?' says Edmée. 'Yes,' says Ukla, 'life almost certainly comes from the stars. I'm working on the surface. Any stones must come from space, because there's nothing around here but snow. If you find one, then you must give it to me.' (If she ever comes back here, she will bring along some stones, she will put them in her pockets, then scatter them about, like Tom Thumb beneath invisible trees.) 'You can't imagine what can be found in the snow. Ten metres down, the smoke from the start of the industrial revolution. At three metres, the ash of the Solfatara. Stick your arm in up to your elbow, and you'll pick up the remains of the World Trade Center. But if you dug much deeper, deeper even than our glaciologists, then you'd discover prehistoric climates, the evaporation of the primitive oceans and the scents of the forests that covered Gondwanaland!' Edmée tries to hear whether the television has been switched on in the video room. 'It's like a tree,' says Ukla. 'You slice through the snow, and its rings tell you how old it is. There are sometimes meteorites in there. Meteorites from the beginnings of the universe.' Edmée finishes her tea and stands up. Where to go? Where are we? What day is it? What can she do? Up there, they will soon be landing on Mars. Mid-January is what they said. That will pass a bit of time.

The landscape rotates around Pete Tomson, and us with it. The huge din of his footsteps – crunching snow, rustling dry-suit – his breathing, the beating of his arteries. The massive disturbance caused by his very presence. By the heat he gives off. The tingling he feels in the nape of his neck, the open eye above him, this constant sun, this end-less day here. The radiance broadens out, the snow scintil-lates around him, an utterly white mist of crystals . . . In two minutes' time, he will not be able to see anything any more. He hurries along, it is cold, the noise gets louder, panting, his own footfalls, the furnace in his throat – the luminous mist rises to a man's height, if he raised his arms and opened the eyes in the hollows of his palms he would see, up there, he would be free . . .

Shapes surround him, whispering. If Peter claps his hands, they fade away, blur, re-form further off . . . Stop kicking at nothing. Someone's calling. Someone's crying out, a female voice, extremely clear. It isn't Edmée. Edmée is the name that leaps to Peter's mind, but it isn't her. It's someone else, someone calling out for help. Just stop kick-ing at nothing, they're going to realise that you can see them, stop covering your ears, you can hear them and they're going to surround you for ever. A ghost attack – like a heart attack, a nervous breakdown, climatic distur-bances and solar storms, Murphy's law and a price to pay. That's what happened to Scott. He doesn't say a word about it in his diary, for fear of sounding insane, but dur-ing their entire journey they underwent similar attacks, their sledges were followed by a ghost convoy. Scott fell into the vortex of time and freak weather conditions, while Amundsen sped along in the sun.

The mist releases its grip slightly. They want to bargain. To suggest what – a pact? What were you thinking of, coming here? What did you expect? To see yourself from a distance, a tiny point on the surface of the snow? To mea-sure your insignificance on the deadest land apart from Mars? To dissolve into the mist, to split into atoms and vanish? *This is the way.* They're opening their arms to you.

They have been expecting you. They'll tell you what you need to know.

A single white shape is standing there, staring into the distance. Peter walks towards it. That's what you risk by leaving your footprints in the snow. That's what you risk by never phoning your family. Peter walks on towards what is left of his sister and mouths these two syllables: 'Clara? Clara?'

The medic is smoking and staring into space. Jan Perse is listening to music on his headphones. Claudio is looking at the wind turbine through the one glass window. The Finn is playing patience. No one pays any attention to Peter, the routine continues its course around the clock, *so apparently I am now the invisible man*, he removes, *zip*, the top of his dry-suit and crosses the living quarters like us ghosts, as silently as rolling marbles.

Ukla the astrophysicist wonders how all these people pass the time when they aren't working. It's as if they were constantly on call. Or conducting a vigil. Do they sleep at night? He can't. He feels terribly lonely, lonelier than he has ever been before on this planet. Is it a sort of initiation ritual? He would just like to have a decent conversation with someone. He's the only scientist to have come in the Caterpillar convoy with the workmen. It must be because he hasn't finished his doctoral thesis yet. But let's not get off the subject. It will be another twelve weeks and three days before Léopold Ukla, of Abidjan City, will be able to hug Maxime and Suzanne Ukla in his arms again. *God bless them*. All the same, this tea has warmed him up a bit. Fresh courage to go out again. Shoes. Shell boots. This awful light. Draw a circle with a radius of five metres, at $2\pi r$.

With two one-metre-deep circles per week, he would really be jinxed if he didn't come across one or two grains of stardust. Then he could finally round off his thesis. Léopold Ukla leans on his spade, breathes hard and sees Suzanne Ukla running towards him, followed by Maxime Ukla in shorts – they'll catch cold. Léopold drops his spade and embraces nothingness. Is that the angelus bell? It's the generator's alarm crying wolf again. Does he have to follow instructions and take shelter at once? Or stay with his spade here and weep? It's only five o'clock. Four more hours before link-up time and being able to talk to them.

The alarm. Edmée half opens the Velcro slit and looks at the sky long enough to burn her retinas. Where is Mars? There are never any stars in this place. The moon, sometimes, when the lighting permits; the white night and a relaxing moon, which proves that we are still on Earth. The alarm stops. He was quick again. What does she usually do at this slack hour of the day? She can't remember. She has found something to do in the morning: scrape off the frost. At one, they have lunch. Then nothing else happens. They can always try to have a nap. Then it's teatime. What has she done, these past few days, after tea? She must have read a book, or had a chat. Cleaned up her booth a bit, before the evening procession. Cleaned the lenses of the projectors. A spot of laundry in her private shower. On the estate, it was simple: she went cycling, she had a bath, she waited for Samuel to come home. She let the hours drift by. How to integrate these two lulls in time, here and on the estate? When it was not too hot, she cycled out to the museums . . . blasts of hot air, blasts of hot air over her bare arms, and the little stabs from the sprinklers, as she passed under them on purpose . . . the poignant smell of the grass

. . . so green . . . Standing in front of the Rothkos, time did not flow, instead it spread out like a lake, swelling. She just had to stand there, trust the Rothkos, and you really were at the centre of the world. You forgot you were in Houston, in the provinces of the planet. From time to time, a car drove past with a discreet swoosh . . . You had to come this far, between the laid-out lawns, the empty avenues, the houses of white wood, as far as the museum . . . Through the noise of the sprinklers, the purr of the air conditioning . . . the huge bay windows . . . the waves of heat across the tarmac and the grass . . . the impeccable emptiness towards the South where the Rothkos slumbered, where the Rothkos quivered in their sleep.

Edmée waits for the link-up. In Scott's diary, there is a section about their routine during winter, before setting off. At ten to nine, the beds were made, at nine they ate porridge, then cleared the table, tidied up a bit and pre-pared their equipment for the expedition, at one they had lunch, and then, weather permitting, they exercised their ponies and did some gym . . . after that, in the evenings, they sang songs and took it in turns to give lectures about their areas of knowledge . . . and, on Sunday, there were prayers and ablutions . . . Months and months of night, until the day came up and, *off and away!* they patriotically set out towards the ice and death. *Amundsen was here first*, written in ghost letters on the trampled snow of the Pole.

Here, the aim is less clear. They all busy themselves in their own ways, the scientists as well as the others. He said that he had to order more gaskets. He at least seems to take his job seriously. What about her, does she do her work properly? For instance, does she take too much satellite time for herself? What do his colleagues say to Samuel? In Houston, when she used to call him at work, the house-to-NASA contact was enough to form a bell jar over them, and their words echoed around inside it agreeably, softly and roundly, like balls of moss, a moss of understanding, of fusion, how to put it? . . . Except, that is, for children. Nothing she plans turns out right. They do not communicate any better here. The distance does not seal their bell jar any better. It's the frost perhaps, the cracks made by the frost. A winter of distance. After all this time, how long, fifteen years, all her adult life. Why is she thinking about that? Like in the 3-D game he enjoyed playing (what did they used to do in the evening? She's forgotten so much that it's as if amnesia is filtering down here along with the light), that game where you have to say the right sentence to the right character at the right time (unreal life is in Houston, real life on this continent), otherwise the characters form a circle and pull funny faces, and you are sent back to the beginning of the scenario. It's the same here. She has quickly learnt to adopt the right tone during the chatter in the living quarters, and them with her, they have the right attitude and the right words, play it fast and well, act out her role as the only woman in the centre of a continent. Except with him, of course, but he is always off in his corner. Which role would he play in Sam's 3-D game? Edmée Blanco waits for the link-up.

Time has taken the form of a stretched rope, with tight knots, close together. On each knot, time stumbles and something happens to us ghosts. Our strange bodies, with the density of uranium and hydrogen, go tense, then relax, grow heavier, then lighter, split open, spin round . . . on one side, and on the other, Edmée's ghosts, Peter's ghosts, with the South Pole as a landmark. Our bodies crack. We are cut in half. The booth is packed with static electricity. *Crack!* A blue/white flash when Edmée folds her sleeping bag. Tidy it away, fold the bed back as a couch, Edmée now offers tea to her holophoners, she has taken a small kettle and some cups from the kitchen. The world is divided into two: tea drinkers and coffee drinkers. This is the point she has reached with her thoughts. The booth is buzzing. Can't wait until the link-up, other scenery, other voices, even thousands of kilometres away, Vladivostok, Tallinn, Milan and Singapore, something, a siphon, other climes . . .

The rope of time has become vertical. She resists, physically. The tiny knots, swallowed one by one, form a second spinal cord in Edmée's body: upright vertebrae of time. For weeks now, Edmée's body has been: dry throat + perspiration + cold extremities + hardened muscles (the daily scraping of the satellite dish) + conjunctivitis (slight ophthalmia) + contextual amenorrhoea (loss of day/night references). Now there are solid, hard seconds stacked up on one another. When the link-up starts, when the blue/green sparkle of virtual space flashes in her booth, Edmée almost runs to remind Peter about his urgent phone call. But a file appears, marked 'Mars', and she supposes that they have done it, they have got there. The download takes twelve minutes. The images are immediately transferred to the living quarters.

First, there is a luminous red decompression chamber, a swoop – the swinging of the cameras floating down on their parachutes. Two of the four are lost – lenses down in the thick dust, another is stuck at an acrobatic angle against a rock (image at about ninety degrees, the Martian soil seen vertically); but the fourth one is filming the module head on. It descends slowly . . . The balance between its

descent and Martian gravity has been calculated carefully
. . . *For the first time in the history of humanity* . . . a permanent
base is going to be set up on Mars! In fact, Peter stood no
chance of being recruited for the mission, but all the same,
he is feeling nervy, he digs his nails into his palms, this
isn't like him at all, he breathes in, once, twice . . . all this is
going to put back his phone call, there is still another nine
minutes of the file. The commentary is incomprehensible,
they might at least have got hold of another file, from
NASA and in English, for example, they are really being
treated like shit here, when you think that the entire planet has already seen these pictures, except them, of course,
because of the wait for the satellite, them and the last four
Innuit without cable TV and the last dozen Papuans . . .
Peter glances at Edmée. She's sitting next to the Imp and
looking very concerned. How slow these last few metres
are. It's as if invisible wires are holding the module above
the red surface. Are those ridges of rock over there? The
dial reads minus ninety-eight degrees C, enough to freeze
them off completely. Deafening silence in the living quarters. A film in slow motion, a film of nothing in particular,
of gilded metal above a powdery surface, vertically in one
picture, horizontally in the other, the other two pictures
being a very dark red, verging on black. Apparently,
Martian dust is as soft and deep as virgin snow. The camera that is filming the right way up is showing maybe a
porthole, and through it there are maybe some shapes
moving about, someone waving hello perhaps? But the
programme is turning it all into 3-D, and the eye cannot
follow any more, unless you imagine it, remake it all yourself. The commentator is getting worked up. Obviously,
they are only going to get this one take of the landing, and
Peter's fingers are itching, press 'Fast forward' and let's

get this over with! The module is about to touch down, at last. Edmée is crimson in her dry-suit. Her eyes are open wide and she seems to be struggling. This impression of knowing what she is thinking. That she would prefer failure and disaster, if only it would go more quickly.

And this heat. Enough to make you faint. Whatever can Mars be really like? Is it really red? . . . Is that because of the distance, the diffraction of light, or whatever? Head spinning, faintly nauseous . . . The commentator's shot up an octave: the module is touching down, nothing in particular is happening. A cloud of red dust rises, forms a sphere, which stays there, like a balloon . . . It's not like the Earth, gravity is very weak. Everyone in the living quarters claps. We clap, too, our emissaries have gone up there with them. We are also born on Mars. The module can still be seen, the sort of chocolate wrapper that covers it is shining . . . And now? The commentator's voice stutters. And in the living quarters, there is a rhythmic sound, *hic-ops hic-ops*, Edmée has got hiccups. Peter stares at the remote control: put it on 'Fast forward' by telekinesis. Apparently, the voice is now trying to fill the void: the syllables sound more detached . . . longer . . . The tone is hesitant . . . there are now gaps between the transitions . . . during the pauses, there is audible doubt . . . that's it, everyone in the living quarters is starting to catch on. Peter and Edmée exchange a look . . . They still have not heard from the astronauts. A vibration, perhaps, runs across the chocolate wrapper. In the second picture, at ninety degrees, you can just make out a door, if you bend your head sideways. Is there banging behind it? It looks as if the module is on vibrator mode, like a mobile phone with its ring tone turned off. The commentator falls silent, then starts up again. About every ten seconds,

Edmée mumbles 'I'm sorry' after each of her hiccups. Chairs creak. Lighters appear, cigarettes are lit. We start up a centrifugal motion and regroup around a kernel of laughter. The module lists, is listing more and more. Slowly, its lateral legs leave the Martian surface. It leans, keels over . . . and comes to rest on its side.

Dust, a sluggish cloud. Now the sideways picture is straight, and the straight picture sideways. It is hard to follow what is happening. A line of puzzlement appears between Edmée Blanco's eyes, and Peter Tomson notices that she is intensely pretty. Consternation mumbles throughout the living quarters. Peter cannot take his eyes off Edmée. Is it because of the golden gleam of the capsule? The beautiful redness of the dust, which is irradiating her cheeks? A 3-D redistribution of her image in the moving light of the catastrophe? She smiles at him. No one is paying any attention to them. Jan Perse and Claudio are standing either side of the module, leaning over it. Soon, like children, they will stretch out their hands to touch it, to set it upright. The others open beers and sigh. They talk: apparently the module has tipped over on to its door. The Imp reckons they need a good can opener, but his joke falls flat. The red dust keeps tumbling down, while an unknown wind scatters it in waves. The image goes out: the twelve minutes are over. People are saying that the oxygen supply in the module will only last twenty-four hours, or maybe forty-eight. Jan Perse diagnoses a breakdown in the circuitry. He appeals to Edmée for confirmation. After all, her husband does work for NASA, doesn't he?

Peter stands up. He is not going to make his phone call this time. That would not be a good idea. It can wait till tomorrow. We stand up after him, *whoosh!*, splitting our mercury mass of ghosts between him and Edmée. And those of us who stay with Edmée lay our heads on her shoulder and watch Peter as he leaves. Because it is in our nature to distort shapes, our veils are sacks full of trouble . . . Delays make us grow, we float in unreason . . . We like to mix things up, to replace one word with another, that is our vocabulary. Navigators of reciprocities, smugglers on sentimental seas; misunderstandings exchanged blow for blow.

They hold a funeral service for the Martian astronauts in front of the NASA headquarters. A pre-recorded news flash. Edmée looks for Samuel in the crowd, but there are too many faces, and 3-D makes groups look unfocused. What is wonderful is the park: an infinity in their living quarters. Everyone seems to be having an attack of claustrophobia, their hands playing with the foliage, as they stroll across the images of lawns, they would so like to breathe in the scent of the flowers. During the minute's silence, they gather together in front of the President, who has his hand on his heart. You can hear the sound of the wind, the trees soughing, birds singing. The automatic sprinklers pour out their manna. The world makes its noises. The heat forms beads. The cool breeze freshens brows. The sky is blue, humid, heavy, dense, sombre . . . To sit down for just a second on that grass and breathe, trail your hand through its blades . . . What was that like? Reconnect with the old world.

But such a world has never existed. Edmée remembers that now. She has escaped from heaps of useless effort. Here, she is light. She likes the cold. She will see trees again later, and sit down on the grass once more. We fold up our blankets of nostalgia again. The Martian module reappears as a final homage, splattered with dusty redness

. . . Adjust the image, a reflex in Edmée's body, redefine those atrocious contours, join together this body, which is standing up, and that body, which has stayed seated . . . In the feverish space in between, Edmée waits, and we wait with her; in the emptiness of the space in between, she encounters us, and ignores us.

III

If black is the absence of colour, the backdrop to the stars, what's stretched across the frame of the universe, then white is the fusion of nothing. All colours mingle there, until the prism is shattered. We can hear thoughts, reverberating in the distance – as if we could see them, far away, Peter and Edmée, their echoes reach us after a moment's delay . . . since this morning, now growing endless, as if they were drifting away . . . We know that this is untrue, that it doesn't exist, they're just mirages, herds, dreams, sea waves, forests. But then you can see the tops of the trees swaying, and some even claim that they can smell the potent odour of inhabitable land.

An urban freeway runs beneath the windows of Edmée's kitchen. She can see the window, and can see herself too, in that dressing-gown Samuel gave her; she can see herself from the back, and in profile at the same time, both inside and outside herself, from the viewpoint of dreams, of ghosts and sometimes of memories. But she can't see the expression on her face. She would like to look out of the window, but there's that freeway. She'd never realised before how close it is, so close that it rubs up against the glass pane as it passes by in reinforced concrete and the wheels of juggernauts shudder against the sill, so near you could get your head crushed. Fortunately, the view from the bedroom hasn't changed: the square fountain is still there, calm and blue. Edmée goes down into the fountain and her dressing-gown becomes heavy. The Higgins children's school books are scattered across the surface. She has the strength to pick them up and put them out to dry. The water is deliciously warm, and a little cooler deeper down. The pressure rises. The farther down she goes, the tighter her dressing-gown becomes, she can scarcely breathe and her temples are throbbing. It's because of a lack of oxygen, the glaciologists say as they bend over her. With great caution, they are going to attempt a tracheotomy, and it is vital that she does not move. She is strapped down on a table, and they introduce a long, white metal tube into her throat. Covered with the hide of a pony, Imelda Higgins looks on impassively.

Very late at night, or very early in the morning, when everyone is asleep, he can relax at last and have the wash basin to himself: his black, very black stubble, nostrils, lift up one cheek, then the other, just like Mr Gudmundsson. Bags under his eyes, you sleep really badly here, hair ruffled, static electricity at levels never experienced before – any metal object you pick up sends shivers up to your shoulder, *zoom*, in a palpable electrical field. Maybe he has lost weight. Turn to the side, try to picture yourself in 3-D, with those thoughts in that box of brains. Or else floating around him, like an atmosphere. To the right . . . to the left . . . Those ideas, ideas floating there, spreading, moving from head to head, everyone half crazy . . . It's the nothingness, the constant company of the same people, and the circle of the sun, its eye always open, and the utter calm of the elements . . . And the medic, asleep on his feet . . . And the Queen Mum stuffing down the leftovers from dinner while cooking lunch, and the leftovers from lunch while cooking dinner, pancakes, maple syrup, bacon, beef casserole, and even cold pasta, apparently he gets up during the night . . . And the incinolette man, who tells them off like kiddies who can't use their potties properly . . . A few years back, the medic based on the coast armed himself with his scalpel and started screaming, apparently they had to bodge up a straitjacket for him (unless there is one included in the equipment) and strap him down on his bed while waiting for the plane to arrive, which can take ages, especially during winter . . . utter darkness and storms . . . the creaking of the pack ice . . . He had downed the entire stock of morphine and was doing cold turkey in the southern winter . . . The atmosphere can also create stories. They tell them to one other in the evening, in the infernal light, so as finally to darken out that inexhaustible daylight . . . The one about the man found frozen in the snow, his face radiant, arms wide open . . . and the snow had moulded the shape of a second, strange body, but one which had melted, disappeared . . . The one about the Twin Otter that was taking its time about finding the reserve of kerosene, and which lands one year later, with its passengers thinking they had only been lost in the fog for a few minutes . . . That military secret, a colony of king penguins wiped out by a virus, bleeding from their eyes and beaks . . . Nocturnal singing; innumerable traces of circular objects landing; and the flag of the loser, Scott, still to be seen fluttering when you approach the Pole . . .

The season advances and the sun declines; with your arm outstretched, it has maybe dropped by the width of your fingers along the horizon. Enough to lose a few degrees, it is now minus forty-seven at night. Pete Tomson, clean shaven, goes for a stroll outside. The sun drills into his eyes. Sunglasses. The sky looks nearer, off white, matt and opaque, ringing like the inside of a bell. The purr of the generator, the acrid smell of the incinolettes . . . Echoes from the building site, compressors, electric screwdrivers, the occasional voices of the night shift, sounding unclear because of the distance and the frost. Thick steam rising from his clothes . . . Dull sounds, brake shoes . . . Edmée now lives permanently in her radio booth. Peter could also put a bed in his boiler room, he has been considering the idea for the last few days, ever since Edmée made the move. But he is a man, and so has no excuse for going it alone. And that sun, like a medal hung on a nail.

Below Edmée's tent, which is inflated by the warm air, we breathe out shapes. We surround Peter so closely, that it is almost as if he is there, standing in front of the tent, thanks to us. But even if we wanted to push him inside, what passes for our hands would go straight through him. We would stumble through his body, while some of us would stay stuck inside. The warm air vibrates beneath the canvas. Peter is so close that he can feel on his frozen eyelashes the warm draught coming through the imperfectly closed fastenings. He undoes the Velcro on his glove, as slowly as possible, but it still goes *scriitch . . . scriiitch*, unless we are just mixing events up for the fun of it. Like a sudden turn in the wind, the maritime din of the building site intensifies . . . booming out . . . Peter takes off his glove. He removes his silk mitten, undoing the poppers, *pit pit pit*. We pummel the ghost of Herzog and make him eat his own stumps. Whether we want it or not, Peter's hand is now bare.

He raises it. He looks as though he is going to take an oath. The cold is already biting into his epidermis, hardening his nails and freezing the blood in his phalanxes, but

Peter Tomson, with the tip of his index finger, gently opens the flap of the canvas tent.

Edmée receives a blast of air and turns round. Everything is ready. The table is laid. She counts the places over and over again. There seems to be one missing. Samuel brings in the enormous Thanksgiving turkey. There will be plenty for everyone. Samuel's head is at a strange angle to his neck, and he is staring up at the ceiling, his chin up. This does not prevent him from eating. The guests are all there, sitting round the table: the Imp, Jan Perse, Imelda Higgins and the Headcase. Edmée counts them again, her head spinning. She just has to keep moving, that's all, a little further and she will be out. There, escaped. She is on the patio of a very beautiful abandoned house. The patio leads out to a garden. The ground is paved with red bricks, carefully laid on their narrower sides. Cubic tubs have been placed at regular intervals, each of them containing a tree. The foliage joins up and forms the roof of the patio. Edmée wanders between the tree trunks.

Warm air. Warm air on a cold hand, warm air on an eye drawing near, blinking. Only the extremities of Edmée are visible. Everything is blue, with yellow rays. Blue canvas pierced by the yellow sun. A blue sleeping bag, hair emerging from it. White steam around her hair appears, disappears. The air whistles. The generator rumbles on, only Peter and we can hear it. Metallic gurgling from the building site. At the bottom of the sea. The submarine world. And Peter and Edmée are on the surface. Now only a ghost could slip between his hand and the split in the canvas. Peter's fingers harden – she is asleep – he pulls the flap a little further back. We blow into Edmée's hair. She turns on to her back.

Sparkles. Peter can see, as though glimpsing a night landscape under a lightning flash, two pale blue eyelids. The red tip of a nose. Hazy hair, with a white arm folded over it. The synthetic crackling of the sleeping bag. We splutter. The most beautiful woman the snow has brought. Let it come. Let the snow come, with its magnetic storms and shared ghosts. And the songs in the waves from the building site, in its whistling. And the heavy-footed herds and their bells, *la la*. The opening is narrow, and the rays of the sun make the shadows darker and the light clearer. Edmée's face forms a pale puddle, continued by her arm, like spilt milk. The top of her shoulder is bare, just the tip, and then there is the sleeping bag. A mermaid. A mermaid's tail. *A mermaid is all I need*. Peter's hand is freezing and very, very hot. Sweat is pouring from his face and freezing instantly into a white mask.

The alarm rings.

We fall silent.

He draws back, the light weighs down on him. In the entire landscape, there is just this tiny pocket of shadows . . . a resting place for the eyes, for the body . . . and sheltering here would be . . . so relaxing . . .

Peter Tomson is cold and his underclothes are soaked. He has stayed outside too long. Walk straight ahead, towards the generator, through the cold and the snow – another sort of calm.

We confer together, we choose our abodes. Those who follow Peter shift off towards the generator; those who stay with Edmée weave plaits in her hair. We have always been here. We, the ghosts of Edmée and of Peter, are like mercury. Our fragments join up, gravity unites us; then we scatter.

Passing from sleeping to waking – HHHHH. If her vocal cords had started to vibrate, Edmée would have screamed.

Sore throat. The dry air and that metallic taste of high altitudes in her mouth. The generator is bawling. She does not know who or what magnetises these fluxes, keeps them under this bell jar and prevents them from spreading. It resonates in her brain. Migraine. (A glass of water – that flat taste of lukewarm, defrosted water, like drinking your own saliva.)

There were two dreams. One unbearable, the other familiar. And someone standing in front of the tent and holding their breath. The air was whistling. Samuel sat down to eat and Imelda Higgins was there, surrounded by animals or spectres. A menagerie, a chicken run. Five children whistling, we shall not be born. Singing, we shall not be born. Five non-children not to be born, for all time. Quick, get up. Edmée opens the flap, sees Peter walking away across the snow. Walking away, as though walking away from here, across an arc of ten or twenty paces, before turning towards the heating system.

The world drifts slowly. The silvery disk of the wind turbine's arms . . . which does not mill the air as much as draw your eyes . . . That is why the mission only lasts a few months, except at the Russian base, but they fuel themselves on vodka, and on the coast, but they have the sea . . .

He would be welcome. No one would be more welcome than him. If he turns round, she will wave to him. And if he does not turn round, she will send him a messenger, a dream messenger, to tell him that, yes, she'd like to, too, that would be just fine.

A bed of shadow under the great sun. We fall silent. The voice of the ice rattles its crystals, in the frost, in space. We fall silent. Our silent voice in space and frost. Silent repetition since the beginning. She's seen him. *Elle l'a vu. Hiiiss.*

117

Chuuut. Huhhhhh. Whiiiistle, in the frost and the crystals, the silent voice from the beginning. A bed of shadow under the great sun. Then the great white sea. Edmée is awake.

Bodge up another gasket. When he fixes it at one side, it blows on the other. But this evening, he will order more gaskets. He will have one thing less to worry about. Really cold outside. You breathe in icicles. Your breath crystallises at once, rustling as it falls on your anorak. Incredible. Only the frost finishes anything here. Completes its job, perfects it, takes it to its conclusion. The frost which is rising up his thighs, which will soon get to his stomach, which will force him back inside in a few minutes' time, back with the others. She must be naked in her rustling sleeping bag, at least her shoulders were. She packs her bags somewhere, she gets on a plane. Naked. He forces himself to dress her mentally, she was of course fully dressed when she took the plane, then the ship, the ice-breaker from Ushuaia; while he, at the same instant, packing in Húsavík, bus, Keflavík, plane, London, then Singapore, that ridiculous heat, then Sydney, then New Zealand, plane, coastal base, plane again, and here, at last . . . and Edmée running towards him and dropping her suitcase, *boom*. Each of them has the ribbon of their journey at their backs. Right around the planet. That makes quite an uncoiling. With arrows pointing this way.

It is geographical. It is geometrical. It is very simple. Peter Tomson will have another thing less to worry about. The sound of a forest in his ears. In his eyes, a wandering circus with giraffes and elephants: a ship, an ark pitching on the horizon; and bears, dancing to the music, and harlequins walking on their hands. The sun is linked to the

118

ground by a semicircle, a rainbow, but a white one, an arc of pure light which draws it downwards, striving to crack the ice. Peter would like to soak up the entire landscape. He spins around. Encompass it, at once, understand – the entire landscape. The air, sun, surface. This landscape inhabited by them alone, this non-place, this incredible non-place, air sun surface. Inhabited by them alone. Crevasses and cracks, and the desire to take it all in, infinity, by quite simply standing here. Because measuring it is impossible. Because cataloguing, mapping or describing it is impossible. Become porous, let yourself be snatched away by the space that is digging out a motionless place here, and fails to set in motion an event, a jolting machine, only because of his footfalls, his very own footfalls. Leaps in time, *crunch boom*. Like on the Moon with Armstrong. *Ding dong*, time starting up on the Moon. One small step for me. Virgin snow, the desire to print your mark there, to initiate something in that direction, where nothing has ever happened.

Peter spins round and round, and those of us who are following him turn like tops. The white/blue ribbon of the landscape is broken by the slight intrusion of the radio booth. Could he have been spotted? Just standing there? The snow in front of the door is more trampled down than elsewhere, like a blue basin. If she was curious enough to study footprints . . . All their boots are identical, but what about their sizes? 1969, first man on the Moon. The astronaut with the name of a jazz musician. Swing, one small step . . . Stripes in the grey dust. They must still be up there.

We have absolutely no idea about that. How to extract ourselves from this atmosphere with which we have surrounded the world? We are indifference made non-flesh.

We mingle together and centrifuge one another, how to distinguish among us between those who have lived, and those who have remained in limbo? Between those who know something, and those who know nothing? Our disguises and appearances cut out shapes from the atmosphere, but the slightest breath undoes us, the wind mixes us up again, we shuffle our cards and swap our images, but they are all just as good, *hop hop* . . . Here, where the winds are born, in the southern eye of the planet, here where we rest. Around Edmée, we rest. Around Peter, we rest. Around the building site, we rest. Around the wind turbine, *chip chip*, that harvests the slightest puff of wind, watt by watt building up the small amount of energy required if there is a breakdown, and a Mayday must be broadcast, before everything cracks, breaks open, all data are lost . . . We blow, kindly. It does not cost us much. Ships sink at sea. Wars break out. Families murder one another. But our weather, so far as we know, is random.

Where is everybody? It's as if even the simplest words are losing their meaning; as if 'this evening' refers to indefinite time, as if 'urgent' means 'later', as if a verb in the future describes a completed action and as if a project, a wish, a plain desire, the expressions of will . . . are getting lost, fading away, turning back . . . Edmée can't get back to sleep. She tries to concentrate on Scott's diary. Nothing happens as planned, as Scott planned, but Edmée knows that, she knows how it will end. Scott is forever looking backwards, at the previous expedition, the ghost of Shackleton, instead of looking to the future, at reality and Amundsen. On 9 January, Bowers's watch inexplicably starts going twenty-six minutes slow. As of 12 January, there is an intermittent sensation of sudden cold, which comes and goes irrespective of the actual weather. On 7 February, some of their biscuit supply has mysteriously vanished. Any of today's magazine readers know better than Scott what is happening to him: calories consumed > calories absorbed = weight loss. Scott and his men are slimming down then breaking up. They lose their toes, their noses, their ears and even lumps of their cheeks. And they start wandering through unknown regions . . . beyond the world . . . And they fade, the wind sweeps them away . . .

Edmée rubs her face. My God, if someone had a really good look. If they dug beneath the cairn of snow that marks their graves. A century in the freezer. They would find Scott's face again. And piles of empty tins, the bones and carcasses of the ponies, the biscuit boxes, the abandoned sledges . . . Everything they left behind must be somewhere, under the snow . . . If she had only imagined, if someone had only told her that she would have so much time to read here! . . . She sits up, puts on a tee-shirt and fiddles with the mouse of her computer. Doodles on the screen. Click on the 'Globe' file and bring up the planet in 3D. Place the hologram in the middle of the booth and click on 'Rotation'. A magic lantern, ochre earth and blue seas . . . The white patch of the Pole beneath . . . A continent as big as Europe. *All I needed*. She lies back down, lets herself drift . . . Daylight, outside . . . the white night . . . With her eyes closed, the world is red. The light is so strong that, even in her tent, she can see the insides of her eyelids, their network of blood vessels, and the reddish orange of her translucent skin. The inside of the body is red, except for the entrails, which are bluish. The red is still there when she opens them. What do you do when you do nothing? And where is the centre of the world? These questions were not born here, she has brought them with her, from the estate, even from before that, from the Lego in the house in Bordeaux . . . A small amount of night . . . she would give several days of her life for just one night . . .

Of course, it is an ocean. An ocean of frozen nothingness. The white crust gives way beneath Peter's boots; below there is also nothingness, powdery nothingness trapped beneath ancient snow, *crunch crack*, a meringue of nothingness cooked in the cold. From Edmée's tent, a beaten track leads to the wind turbine. Her little to-ing and fro-ing, like a hibernating rodent (the zigzagging tracks of stoats, and those spotless birds identified thanks to their take-off, *flak flak flak*, the black line under their wings, where has he seen that before?). The virgin snow beyond. See the sun turn. And dissolve, as a vanishing point appears between the body and the Earth. Peter looks up at the sky, where stratus clouds are drifting gently, coming from the four cardinal points and cancelling one another out here, at their point of contact; as if the Pole were siphoning the sky . . . as though they were melting in the blue, or as if the blue was in fact born from their melting . . . You could be upside down. Your feet in the blue and your head in the white. With a sky of virgin snow and azure to walk on. We stand aside; Peter passes by. His footprints are already there, *crack crunch*, he just has to slide his feet inside them, he is light, shoes and shell boots, he goes towards Edmée's booth.

If nothingness has a centre, then Houston is at the centre of nothingness, with Douglastown on its outskirts. The yoga lessons were held twice a week in the estate's Community Centre. On Tuesdays and Thursdays. It was hard to say if yoga really did Imelda Higgins any good, but at least it got her out of the house. And given that Edmée was talked about for being so idle – a husband and qualifications, but no children or job – or, perhaps, because Edmée really was a good person, whatever, Edmée had offered to look after the kids on Tuesdays. In fact, at that time of day, the youngest was having his nap – though you had to rock him all the time, so one arm was out of action – and there were only four other Higgins kids left to deal with. The one who was twenty months old could always be put in his playpen, the one who was three could be stuffed with biscuits, but the next one up was epileptic and was not to be excited under any circumstances; as for the eldest, he refused to talk to anyone except his mother. Unless Edmée (it is two years ago already, the first time she has counted) is mixing up their symptoms and hierarchy, being neither their mother nor their tombstone. There had been talk of Edmée giving the eldest one French lessons (what was his name?). He must have been seven or eight at the time, since he was nine when it happened. This was one of the few things Imelda could not deal with on her own: everything to do with school, the piano lessons, the maths, the art and the Spanish, and even the basketball, and it was always her who was by the square fountain organising ball games and prisoner's base, tricycle rides or sack races – but not French. Of course, the attempt had aborted rapidly, given that the eldest Higgins never opened his mouth.

Samuel had warned her not to get involved, that it was none of her business how the Higginses brought up their children. And he was right. Apparently, she was pregnant again when it happened. That Tuesday, Edmée had called to say that she could not look after the children, and she had gone to do yoga at the Community Centre instead of

123

Imelda. She had breathed from her stomach while going *Om*. None of the other neighbours wanted to take their turn any more. Only Jason Stuart sometimes gave them his leftover pizzas, which made one fewer meal for Imelda to plan, and the Wilkes kids mowed their lawn. Dr Spry, the paediatrician, dropped by to see them from time to time. So you couldn't say that no one had tried, or were not attempting to keep things at a sustainable level. That Tuesday, at around a quarter past three, Imelda Higgins ran a bath in the large jacuzzi in the upstairs bathroom, while still cradling the baby. It was a stiflingly hot July afternoon. Despite the air conditioning in the yoga room, just one single ray of sun on your body was enough to make you break out in a sweat. Still holding the baby, Imelda Higgins helped the other four get undressed. Apparently, the eldest refused. She took him to one side, while the other three were already playing in the water obediently, and knocked him out with the hairdryer. Then she plugged the hairdryer in, turned it on and dropped it into the jacuzzi. She dragged the eldest bodily up to the water and pushed him in. It is not known at what exact moment Imelda Higgins freed up her arm by throwing the baby out of the window. What is certain is that it was before she slit her wrists lengthwise. The baby fell on to the soft grass, which grew luxuriantly under the sprinklers. He was the only one of the Higgins children to survive.

What is he doing, back outside that tent closed with Velcro? Can you still be afraid on a continent where so many 'conquerors' have died? We cast our words at him like shards of bone. Maybe it is because he is living according to the disjointed rhythm of his generator. He is losing the plot. When he manages to sleep, the few dreams he has are more vivid than his daily life. In his dreams, it is night time. The possibility of real rest is there. But now he is in front of . . . this door of canvas, he does not even know what to call it, or how to knock on it. So he scratches at it with a glove. He senses that he is smiling, and this is cracking his frozen cheeks. *What are we going to talk about?* The question whistles in his ears, along with the air from the tent, and his heart beats faster. Mars, or Scott's diary. Who cares? The astronauts . . . talk about the dead, that passes the time. There are only two places to sit, the sofa-bed and the chair. Peter is abruptly aware of his body standing in front of Edmée's body lying on the bed. She observes: 'It's too late to phone.' He agrees: 'I know.'

There, everything has been said now. The tent has puffed up to bursting point in this endless second. Peter and Edmée are huge. They fill up the tent and the entire continent, they spill out over the seas. A centrifugal force is chasing us away – they are taking up the entire space, they want to do without us! Edmée moves her hand a few centimetres, space folds back, the tent bends, canvas against canvas, the dimensions curl up – we resist: we can speak for them! But Edmée has placed her hand on Peter's thigh, she leans against him, Peter bends down . . .

We hang on to the guy ropes of the tent, a phantom blizzard is ripping apart our immaterial bodies – *'It was love at first sight'*, *'amour pour toujours!'*, *'strangers in the night!'* – a chicken run of ghosts, a cackling of feathers and plumes – *'us! us! '* – owls shooed away in all directions, sent flying, out of here!

Silence. Edmée releases her hands. They slide down the slopes and plains, two little horses going at their own pace, freely over Peter's body. As for Peter, he still holds his hands back, clenching his fingers in the hollows of his palms. If he lets them go, he is sure Edmée will be naked in no time – *patience* – it is his own voice that he can hear, the voice in his head, in his own language – he feels marvellously empty, open and vast, the world is huge, night will fall in a few months, we have all the time in the world – a twelve thousand volt cable runs around the little booth, no one will knock at our door, no car will stop with a screeching of brakes, and the ill wind will not carry us away – we are alone, the air, the future, space have been released and are free, we are perfectly alone, we have nothing to do but look, look to see how we are going to manage – and the luminous globe spins, Asia-Europe-Africa-America, crossed over by hands, napes, mouths, hair, Edmée-Peter-Edmée-Peter – *oooh!* a voice wails again – the chicken run of ghosts, crying out and rejected – Peter, says yes, murmurs yes, rolls yes in Edmée's mouth . . .

But the generator bell rings, and it takes Peter a few seconds to remember his longitudes and latitudes, the snow and the sun, the cold, the frost, his job here and the danger now threatening. He takes a few more to laugh with Edmée, and more to devour her mouth again, to consume her face. Another handful to recover a vertical posture and to let himself be held in her hands. And a good minute to become decent and lace up his boots. Then thirty-eight seconds to stride over to the generator. The ghosts have joined up hand in hand around the booth and are whistling – a few swim upstream in the current of warm air and try to get inside – Edmée ties up her hair, and rinses her face. Alone, deliciously alone, heavy from Peter's kisses, from Peter's body as it fleetingly lay there, heavy. She is sitting up, anchored and heavy, with all the time she needs to take hold of that body, and light with the helium of certainty which is filling her chest, head, entire body – the large, still-warm anorak which he has left behind makes an extremely welcome dressing-gown – she hums as she laces up her boots, she will go and see him at work.

@p1:*'That woman is too good for you!'* the ghosts bawl at the tops of their voices, over the generator's alarm bell, *'It will never work out!'*, Peter shuts it up with a blow from his spanner. Where's the problem? Bugger these gaskets.

The generator is purring. It is mild in here. The floor of insulated metal is warm, three or four square metres are free, enough for two bodies. And so. Here, no one will come to disturb them. A fold forms across the floor . . . a slope . . . Far, far out to sea, the waters swell as though pulled by the tide, a balance is struck between the laws of physics and this phenomenon here: Edmée's body and Peter's body rolling towards each other. Their shared presence makes them immense, fluid yet also massive. Far, far out to sea, a school of whales tries to use its huge mass to fill the gap made by their bodies. Giant squids surge up from the gulches; glaciers calve down their litters of icebergs; tectonic plates thrust up through the surface of the magma: this is the very least that must happen, after Peter and Edmée have joined together, if the physics of the world is to right itself again.

Space is intermittent, pierced by hollows and niches, they tumble into its voids, discover its fault lines which slip between their bodies, multiplying them by two, again and again. Touch sets cells alight, creating bridges between the worlds. E is not P, P is not E. They incorporate what seems like time. Bubbles of daydreams burst in their

127

minds: *circle by circle, we moult and now we are naked. We do not melt, we do not mingle: we touch each other*. No one is there to tell them stories any more – they stamp their feet and chase the entire universe away – *pfut!* the booth is empty. And their choir swells with this resonance of nothingness, this immaculate space. It is only at a distance, outside, in the snow, that the shadows gather. Beneath the perpetual sun, a stage is being set up. Tristan and Isolde, Heloise and Abelard, crucified lovers, Romeo, Juliet, the Prince and the Princess pull faces on the boards. To be left this much out of the reckoning . . . to be disregarded this much . . . the ghosts group together, congregate, become one with this canvas shelter . . .

There is only one place left in the world where they can slip through: Peter's penis. The ghost inside it attempts a final gambit, summoning spectres with people's names, the ill-buried, the specialists in cold. The shelter is ripped open and explodes: their avalanche bursts in through the gap. The *'It can happen to anyone'* would so like to emerge from Edmée's mouth, but bitter mute Icelandic curses are blasting the terrain like grenades. Edmée gets the giggles. Peter summons his blood to the fray. Nothing. Ghosts on the hunt like pointers. Nothing. Peter's brain is on freezer mode. His teeth allow through two or three syllables in some language or another. Edmée's laughter peals out. Space rebounds, elastic and gilded. Things aren't that bad.

Outside, they walk as best as they can. Let the air drift by, breathe. It is four in the morning. The exasperating sun hangs down. Their heads spin, their legs feel like jelly. The extraordinary monotony of their surroundings seems farcical to them. They are dressed in Kevlar, thermal fabric, fleece and leather; and the atoms of nitrogen and oxygen, suspended between them at minus forty-seven degrees C, scarcely move, at the speed they walk. Their mouths are bare, that is all. They draw nearer: extremely cool flesh on the surface and then heat, humidity within. *Click clack* of colliding sunglasses. *'French girls kiss like this,'* a persistent ghost tries to follow them. Peter grabs Edmée's balaclava in both gloves, diving deeper into the naked space. Edmée, her head in rapture, dives into the gap too.

Then they walk on. *'They won't get far'* (two old men of the Pole, muttering on a bench). Ukla the astrophysicist's snow scooter is there, in the middle of nowhere. The key is in the ignition, naturally. A very slight incline in space is enough to send Edmée and Peter spluttering off across the desert. *'No more than twenty minutes!'* it is Peter who speaks, the voice of his conscience has regained control of his mouth – *'Let them all croak!'* – says the voice of Edmée, who has taken control of the scooter.

First, they follow Ukla's tracks, his circular excavations for meteors, and when they reach the last circle, they head due south towards the Pole: about a quarter of an hour's drive in the scooter, or three days' march for Scott. When you live by the sea, you go and look at the sea. When you live by a waterfall, a beautiful view or the gulf of Padirac, you go and look at the waterfall, panorama, gulf. Here, you go to the Pole. You just have to follow the cairns of shovelled snow. The South Pole does not exist, it is mere hearsay, nothingness's centre of gravity, one patch among many on a white map. *Poot poot poot poot*, goes the scooter amid a huge rout of ghosts. Slowly, the sky has started to enclose space. The sky-ground gap closes up, white sky against white ground. Edmée squints. Despite their sunglasses, the whiteout becomes total. She slows down. The horizon has vanished. It is not that the sky and snow have melted into continuous whiteness. No. It is that there is no longer any sky or snow.

'What does the South Pole look like?' Edmée asks, putting the *poot poot* into neutral. 'I think there's a cairn for Scott and Amundsen. Or a big cross to show you're there, like the line at the equator.' Anyway, apart from each other's lips beneath their glasses, and the fluorescent strips on their absent bodies, everything has disappeared. Their voices are flat and dry, no echo can find a footing. They get off. They hold each other round the waist and steady themselves on the scooter. They fall over. Everything is white. They fall into whiteness. If they let each other go, they will vanish. But if they let go of the scooter, they will really be in trouble: with their free gloves, they grip on to the machine tightly. They embrace, knees against the motor. Their saliva freezes in the corners of their mouths; they suck it, they eat each other. It is the first time that two humans have mingled their lips and tongues at the South Pole. History, of course, does not turn over in its cavern. Time only glances back over its shoulder, like an animal raising its snout for a moment from the carcass it is devouring. But it is enough for space to be able to dig out its slopes again, for the world to be tipped slightly out of true.

There, a couple of metres away, a perspective is forming. Enough depth to model an object, the three dimensions of something, a disc, shining without the sun. It is still hesitant . . . its proportions fluctuate . . . the disc takes up the entirety of this recreated space, covering the available area . . . or else, it contracts to a point. Such extreme oscillation sends it spinning. Edmée leans down and it suddenly goes still: it's a watch. What's more, it even looks like a watch from the previous century, from the start of the century, a wind-up watch, but without a strap. Strangely enough, it is warm, as if it had just fallen out of a pocket. And it is going tick tock. The tick tock is gigantic. It bounces, alone against nothing. Edmée checks her own watch, from the twenty-first century: they have now been gone for twenty-six minutes. But the old watch says that it's still four o'clock. It's Bowers's watch.

The only thing to do now is turn back, following metre by metre the trail left by the scooter. Bore out their own space through the whiteness. Their own trajectory, slowly, metre by metre. *Poot poot poot poot*. It breaks apart as they go. It widens but makes no comment. It is a perfect nothingness of nothing. Peter and Edmée start bawling out any old international anthem, *We are the champions*, for instance, what does it matter, only they can hear it. Crazy with joy and nothingness.

'Thieves!' curses Ukla the astrophysicist, whose head has just popped up in front of them. Was it the sound of the motor that got him out of bed? He is fully equipped from head to foot. Claudio and Jan Perse are either side of him. The whiteout disintegrates. The familiar purr of the generator, the rumble of the building site, the clacking of the pulleys in the glaciologist's workshop, everything falls back into place, everything fits back together. 'Shit,' Peter mumbles in his language. 'What time is it?' Edmée asks. It is four in the afternoon. Teatime. Bowers's watch has stopped going tick tock. Edmée can't even find where she put it.

Landscapes of naked bodies: slopes and slants. Irregularities, fissures, pale or brown plains, Peter's dark thigh across Edmée's light thigh. And the gap that enables them to look at each other; the tip of space and time; the arrow that points them out. Mites feed off skin scales; ghosts off psychological ones. They have left them behind as they go. Everything they discover is part of this discovery; what they explore, of the exploration. Their amazement, they accept. Smells, fluids, hairs, tastes – this enormous joy, they accept. P and E do not feel the passing of time. The ghosts are at the door and getting bored; on the verge of getting annoyed.

In the hollow of E's groin, P has a three-quarter view of her vulva, like a face looking away. The colour of the leaves of crumpled skin fluctuates, beige/purple; curtains, hangings, shutters. If he leans more heavily on her thigh, the leaves open, one tautens, the other wrinkles up a little more, and their pearly pink interior is revealed to be almost blue there where, like a highly polished slide, the vagina begins. Narrow at its opening, even though the delta suggests a long median, only the base is split. It is an object of multiple geometries: unfolding the leaves makes them blossom into diamonds, the gleaming oily depths open into a triangle above a cylinder of multiple internal circles – those fortune-telling games, with cups of open or closed paper that girls play with at school; and their games with stretched elastic dividing space into trapeziums between their crossed then uncrossed legs . . .

'What are you looking?' Edmée asks in their international pidgin. The ghost of past prudery drifts by, calm and slow and worthy. A line of hairs decks the fold of the lip, with a flick of his tongue he raises it. A burst of weary blood wanders into his member and he sighs. It's still talking time. The teeth of the vampire hidden in his prick remain solidly in place. Edmée half closes her thighs. With her hand in his hair, she invites him to move further up.

Edmée's blonde hairs, that sombre blondeness that never sees the sun, are now tickling Peter's cheek. The profile of her clitoris stands out, curled and rather sullen. The booth swirls. It's almost as bright inside as out.

From the sofa-bed where they are lying, they can see the Pole head on, below the hologram of the globe which is wrapping them up in its rotations. 'It reminds me', Peter daydreams, 'of the mosses that grow in rings around tree trunks . . . ' – 'And me', Edmée daydreams, 'of a lamb, the foetus of a lamb . . . ' – 'I can see its ear . . . ' – 'And me its nose . . . ' – 'And the amniotic fluid . . .' The Pole passes by, taking their faces and thought bubbles with it . . . Lands with no forests and seas without water . . . animals, trees . . . sounds, silences . . . The fragrance is complete, mucus, spray, fluids. 'One of the tropical crabs with its single claw' . . . 'A brain' . . . 'A cauliflower' . . . they toy with each other, pinching, nibbling . . . When they cannot find the right word in English, they say nothing . . . they turn to shadowplay, a dog, a whale's skull, a long-tailed butterfly. An elephant. A zebra. When the word does not come, they choose another . . . Rhythm . . . Cymbals in motion. Pulsating ventricles. An orchestra, a bear pit. A cell in meiosis. A merry-go-round of ancient horses. 'A barrel organ,' Edmée whispers. *'What?' 'Music.' 'I can hear it too.'*

Peter's penis is lying on his thigh, brown and red and indifferent. His curly hairs form moist spirals, as dense as springs, and extremely black. Edmée extricates his balls and cups them; dark mauve, moving freely below their envelope, in the fluidity of nearly naked glands; organs external from the body, revealed, extraordinary. She toys with them in the palm of her hand, like marbles. It would be nice to force them into her vagina and orgasm as they roll about – but that's just impossible. This skin, so fluid . . .

how it contracts when you squeeze it, how it wrinkles up into coarse ridges, the hide of a young elephant, harsh velvet, and when released, this translucent silk – and the penis rises, lazily, then droops sadly once more below Edmée's lips, as she nibbles at it, amused, worried, courteous – this impotence is making her imagination run riot . . . 'I'm going out,' says Peter. 'I'M GOING OUT!' He would give anything for a highway, streets, a bar, a port, a sea to cross.

The white horizon is overpowering; triumphant invisibility is let loose. Peter urinates, standing up in the snow, his prick at minus forty degrees C, and someone is standing in front of him. Someone or something, with the sun shining through it. As a result, Peter urinates through it. But the someone or something seems impervious: standing there just as Peter is standing there, but only that, just there: a condensed form of whiteness, cosmic precipitation, a milky column, hardly any heavier, or weightier, or more melancholy and desperate and alone than anything else that belongs to this whiteness. Look: a huge mouth is opening. Full of teeth, and filaments and stickiness, blood oozes out – bloodshot eyes appear and, beside them, bleeding ears and, in the middle, a bloodied nose; and, lower down, what looks like a vulva takes shape, ripped apart and ghastly with blood. Peter's hair stands up below his hood so much that he actually feels it as it rises; but it's nothing, because with the flat of his glove he easily smoothes it back down again. *'Fuck you, Clara,'* he says, as calm as can be.

The ship is docked. It can be boarded via the gangplank, thence into a small panelled room where a rather grumpy-looking pharmacist is standing behind a counter and staring straight at everyone who comes through the door. Her fingers are test-tubes, and the electric light shines though the palms of her hands. A billiard table slumbers in the half-light. Men dressed in heavy checked shirts are leaning against the bar, drinking and smoking. They turn round to look at Edmée and Peter. One single, identical face above their checked bodies. 'Let's go out the back way,' says Edmée. The water is smooth, silvery, almost non-existent. You can sense that the sea is just behind the harbour wall; a matt yellow dawn is rising, it smells of sea-weed and ether, the metallic water glints like bronze. At the end of the gangway, there is a hatch where you can place your order. Hands give them a paper bag, marked with the usual green cross, and they have one thing less to worry about. 'In the prow', says Edmée, 'there's a swim-ming pool, I feel like taking a dip.' They walk for ages, slithering, across the boards of a dance floor. At the pool, there are slides, water jets, jacuzzis, children running around, jumping and yelling. 'I'm bleeding,' says Peter. 'We'll make an appointment,' says Edmée. They each take a notebook out of their pockets, seasons are marked out by differently coloured vertical bars, mostly blue and white, dozens of seasons making a wavy ribbon across the pages.

The *scratch* of the Velcro – Peter is back – wakes up Edmée. She says: 'All the same, we'll have to find some condoms.' 'The cold kills infections,' he hazards. 'I wasn't thinking about that.' 'Let's try the first-aid box, then.' They laugh. Season by season, the people who come here have built an imaginary world out of the Lego blocks of absence. I'm just going down to the beach and I'll be straight back. I'll pick you up at the station. I'm going to gather some snowdrops. P kisses the inside of E's thigh. Tender, fatty skin, folds rolling up like granulated sugar. He slides along unchecked smoothness. A word crystallises inside his brain, a word in his language, he cannot hear it, its meaning surges up: *inexhaustible*. His mouth overflows with it on the thigh he is kissing. The little folds are the membranes of her lips, he eats them, absorbs them, lets himself be absorbed and melt into this warm, fatty softness . . . And his mouth draws out pathways on E . . . from the swell of her thigh to her armpit via her ankles and the strip of her diaphragm, the lines cross on E's sex and remain there, taut, vibrant . . . tighter and tighter . . . the inflow of energy swells her vulva, she guides P's hand to untangle the knot, to pull out thread by thread what is tightening there . . .

If the strange word *yes* is a language all on its own, E and P now speak it. Backs, armpits, legs, shoulders, necks, arses, mouths, brows, bellies, phalanges, ilia and popliteal muscles make up penetrable, warm bodies, burning up oxygen, consuming water and carbon. And this delightful anatomy fills the tiny shelter of the booth, a hot air balloon, tie ropes splitting, they look eye to eye . . . sex in sex at last! And they giggle, the entire base must be able to hear all these noises, and they love that idea, no one will be able to talk about illusions or paranoia, and anyway nobody ever does . . .

They know about these pathways, these transformations, they have already followed them, the caresses here that go there, sex turning into a body, and the pleasure both inside and out . . . like thought, inside and outside the body . . . It is neither a discovery nor a shock, just a new magnetic lake . . . Swim in it . . . The pull of the void . . . Introduce your form into it . . . Dive into its waves . . . Into the currents born of transformations, of the space between bodies, shrinking, expanding . . . This is no stunning revelation, it is just the exploration being carried out by pleasure and thought, here and now, in familiar dimensions. The ghosts of yesterday and of tomorrow can always try . . .

I can't think any more is E's last thought before she forgets herself, the things people say, syllogisms, and the way time and space enclose her. Pleasure polarises and images flow in, the lake widens, spreads out, her sex is one point in this lake, an island around which suspension bridges are swaying, this is the last image in Edmée's mind when orgasm snatches her away – even from images – she calls out. In P's mind, oddly enough, Ukla the astrophysicist is repeating again and again an extract from a lecture, the sentence is bouncing back and forth between two sonic mirrors: '*At 10^{34}°C the irreversibility of time breaks down.*' Time spins around itself, slows, changes direction, gives up – P loses the thread, this is happening right now, in this universe, in the cores of suns, of novas, of red giants, at the beginning of the beginning of the Big Bang – before he closes his eyes on a cry, Edmée forming a lake of pale light between his hands.

Their steps are leading them through a large flat. On three sides of it, the city lights swell, grey and yellow, with wonderful fullness. Peter goes over to a window and opens it: far below, a traffic jam is throbbing. Red lights – *I'd forgotten about red lights* – are changing amid universal indifference. Only Peter and Edmée, from their vantage point, notice that everyone is breaking the rules. Pedestrians pass by, blobs seen from above, sometimes behind the rectangle of a buggy. When the window is closed again, the flat is silent. Thin metal columns push the ceiling up to a great height. No partitions or furniture. The full, soft rumble of the traffic jam at the windows makes their solitude palpably delicious. Nothing happens. The dust drifts in the warm, round light. Heat and quiet echo each other, it is warm and calm, all is calm and warm. The heat and quiet rise up the columns with the warm air which slowly lifts up the balloon ceiling. If sleep is a slumbering creature, this is its dream. Outside, the traffic jam is raging. The hooters are blaring, an ambulance or the police are trying to get through.

The alarm is ringing. It must have been ringing for some time . . . They look at each other . . . The place where they come from . . . High above the din, above the sea . . . Time is putting itself back together at top speed, and wailing – *ouiiii* . . . This wailing in their ears, these cries at any time, this was the South Pole. Peter slips on his dry-suit. A remembrance of orgasm grips him, almost as strong as the orgasm itself. Edmée's face . . . Eyes closed . . . Stay there . . . Motionless . . . Where are they? E is next to him, naked, standing. The *ouiiii* is persistently ripping apart the continuity of their bodies. In P's mind, as he drags every movement from his limbs one by one – tie up your boots, put on your gloves – in P's mind there is a persistent image of a *Caterpillar*, its tracks biting through the ice at full power. With its trailer full of food and fuel, in its insulated cabin, they could hold out for weeks in the snow, all the way back to the coast. White nights, the two of them, in the middle of nowhere – and then escape by sea, get themselves repatriated somehow, by the Russians or the Americans . . .

Claudio and the medic are at the door of the dormitory, they watch him go by. Peter shoulders his way through white shapes, routs horses with a kick. No time, no time . . .

A minute to think. A premonition . . . a certitude . . . unfolds inside him, taking the place of his entire body . . . He goes towards the generator, *ouiiii, ouiiii*, but what has been set in motion by his steps is an irreparable variety of time. His body has its double, he can sense the slow destruction going on in there, the sabotage getting worse as he nears it . . . Growing clearer, reaching into the cogs, gripping the entire machine . . . Digging deeper into the circuits . . . The distance increases, the effort he has to put in to making ground releases an opposing force: the *ouiiii* forms a circle around him.

'What's going on?' Edmée has rushed over to join Peter at the heating system, before the others dash there too. They have to shout to make themselves heard, *ouiiii* . . . P is armed with some pliers, he ferrets around in the innards of the machine. E kicks aside the metallic intestines, she has her hands in the pockets of P's anorak and is watching intently, it feels as if the temperature is already falling. The *ouiiii* stops suddenly, questioningly, strangled . . . P victoriously passes a handful of wires to E. 'Phew,' she whistles. The generator shudders. P and E jump, they are on edge, it makes them laugh. Beneath the red hood, split in half like a thorax, some sort of rust has spread through the circuits. It bubbles up around the cracked gaskets, it seems to be oozing from the rubber, a reddish paste has bitten through the pipes. 'Amazing what the cold can do,' says Edmée, soberly.

It is her turn to act. She knows what she has to do, the procedure has been codified. 'Mayday, Mayday,' the emergency channel on her radio, an SOS launched thanks to the energy from the wind turbine. You can hear the motors stopping, the dying away of hisses no one noticed before, giving way to a silence which is unheard on this planet, the silence of a capsule, of inner nothingness. Peter tries to put together some phrases in his mind, an acceptable, correct, apologetic way to tell the others they are going to have to evacuate.

In the isothermic chamber, Peter is in one corner, Edmée in another. There is the greatest possible distance between them. They have been positioned symmetrically: if there were any cardinal points at the Pole, P would be NE and E would be SW. But as the chamber is only six metres long by four metres wide, and is situated at about fifteen kilometres from the Pole, it can be positively stated that the geographical position of Claudio, Jan Perse, the Imp and the glaciologists, the Finn, the Queen Mum, Ukla the astrophysicist, Dimitri the meteorologist, the chief engineer, the site manager and the workmen, plus Peter and Edmée, is ninety degrees south by zero degrees east or west, as you wish, given that you can turn around on a coin here, it all comes down to the same thing.

Edmée doesn't dare look at Peter. If he looks at her, she will smile, and that will not go down very well. A blood bath. They are going to have to watch out, things like that can happen. Ukla the astrophysicist, already horrified by the business about the scooter, will never finish his thesis; the glaciologists will not reach the waters of the lake, the Americans will win the race; in the ancient ice, they will not discover the antivirus to save humanity or the bacteria that could have wiped it out; the White Project will now be a season late, the budget allotted for this year has been wasted and may not be reallocated; the damage caused by the frost will cost a fortune; and if weather conditions are bad, they will have to stay in this shelter for days and days, twenty-four square metres for twenty-four people, eating survival rations and drinking high-energy beverages.

They are sitting in a row, backs against the sides: Edmée, between Claudio and Jan Perse, is trying to breathe as little as possible and hunching her shoulders to take up a minimum amount of space. She wants to urinate – how is that done, are they allowed to go out? It's terribly hot. All these bodies at thirty-seven degrees C, plus the anger, mean they will not freeze to death. It has now been an hour since she launched her 'Mayday'. The local weather is bad, they will have to wait until the depression moves away from the coast, and as a C-130 cannot land here, they will have to arrange a shuttle service with a Twin Otter, only four people per trip, with all the risks that implies, while leaving their equipment here. Their baggage and personal items will be transported in the Caterpillar trucks, as well as what can be salvaged from the ongoing experiments. The Imp is muttering about drill cores with Dimitri. He seems to have lost his sense of humour. If, to kill time, Edmée had to classify them in terms of who looked the most furious, she would put the Imp in first place, then the boss Claudio second. He was the one who broadcast the second 'Mayday' on the emergency transmitter. Apart from the Imp's muttered conversation and a sort of groaning from the medic, the evil whistling of the emergency transmitter is all that can be heard. As for Jan Perse, he has just been out and come back again without asking anyone's permission. There are no incinolettes in the chamber, so what is the protocol? Can they use the urinals in the base? Still, they will have been there for almost half the season . . . seventy-two days. She has only had her periods once. Let's hope that will sort itself out soon.

The medic looks decidedly poorly. He is groaning, and staring into space. The chamber only has a tiny little inspection window, a blue triangle, and they cannot see the wind turbine, just a patch of meteorological sky. The coastal base will keep them informed of the changing weather conditions on an hourly basis . . . Claudio is trying to organise this coming night. Edmée feels a twinge of nostalgia for her power as operator when distributing satellite link-up time. And so, there is not enough room for everyone to lie down. If they have to stay here for several days (Edmée wilts) they will have to take it in turns to sleep. The Queen Mum hands round the survival rations. When he gives her hers, his bright red face, wrinkled and ageless, seems to shift upwards. She manages to accept eye contact: this sudden kindness, this vaguely pink rejuvenation . . . it must be a smile, given away with the biscuits and peanut butter. Edmée's throat feels empty. That sensitive spot ever since she arrived, that permanent sore throat from the cold and the altitude – something seems to slide and run. No, they won't see her cry. She won't give them that pleasure.

Claudio gets to his feet, he motions to the Finn and to the chief engineer . . . they all head straight for Peter. Sitting cross-legged, almost in the lotus position, he doesn't see what's going on, he's going to get himself killed . . . They put on their anoraks, they go out, they take him with them. A blade of cold air . . . The Imp and the three glaciologists are going to sleep first. Everyone shoves up closer against the sides, knees up against their chests. Edmée chews her biscuit silently. Pastry made of water, salt and flour fills her mouth, her head, her chest . . . If she lets herself go, she will burst into tears. Of course they're going to put her in the last plane, to punish her . . . They'll organise that all right, the vengeance protocol must have been codified to death. The air is already oppressive, they should open up, air the place . . . Toxic liquor being shaken and stirred by their breathing . . . A breath in, the simple fact of her chest rising, has a direct relationship with the perceived hatred . . . Space shrinks abruptly under an enormous din – *BANG!* – is it a gun, is there one on the base? Edmée's heart stops – another blast. But it is only the first pipes blowing.

Claudio comes back, and so does the Finn, the engineer; and Peter. They're carrying things, have salvaged something or other, who cares? She shuts her eyes. Head empty. Empty. A colour . . . red. Eyelids, inside the body . . . A contraction of space, *bang!* Another pipe, plug your ears . . . The whole base is going to explode, they didn't have enough time to empty out the fuel . . . Who cares? Claudio's stubborn mass sits back down, she opens her eyes again: Peter looks at her from the far side. An empty corridor takes shape, a channel, a cone . . . Which you only have to follow . . . Impregnable and private . . . No latitude no longitude . . . The memory of what they've just done is red . . . Becomes huge again . . . Central . . . It takes them by their bellies and brains . . . Rises like a giggling fit . . . Please don't laugh, a sense of palpable death . . . Look down . . . Shut up . . . Relocate an orderly, well-oiled world with laws, cycles . . . seasons . . . strangers, nameless crowds, streets . . . All that is left now is a wandering journey . . . geography, distances, delays and diversions, but that doesn't matter, they know all about that, about details, unforeseen events, impatience . . . time and space they know all about, ducking and diving and back again . . . If the cold and the others spare them, it will be just a question of marking a cross on the planet, a place they will choose together. It's material and measurable. Who cares about the rest? They'll know all about that. Escape together, the only us-twos, the world, they'll just know. The South Pole for others. The thermal chamber, without us. The desert that grows, but without us. Mars, and dead children, and suffering survivors, and the hooks of ghosts, without us.

From a split, dark red, folded follicle, a sphere with a diameter of about a quarter of a millimetre drifts away. Decked with numerous cilia, it floats along a corridor full of highly fluid juices, performing whorls that look almost ornamental, with twists, turns . . . upstream, a cloud of corpuscles race onwards, struggling, how can they be counted? Measuring at most sixty microns, wiggling from head to tail, they jostle. They are milky and triangular, while the queenly sphere is more crimson. The centre is closed, within there is just the right temperature, and the corridors we are talking about can only be seen in this light: everything is opaque, and utterly devoid of reason. An isothermic chamber, if you like, but one that is organic and living. One of the little triangles is finding its way through two crimson cilia . . . which separate slightly . . . let it through and *pop!* snap back, closing a solid membrane behind it. In the mingled plasmas, proliferating filaments radiate into star patterns, which are not unlike the aster flower. The triangle and the sphere merge, two spirals entwine: an egg is born. First doubled, then quadrupled, the cells that make it up, with an equal share from P and from E, will in the next few days find a comfortable niche in a mucous membrane, bursting with healthy blood.

In the ice-breaker that takes them home, a good three weeks after the breakdown, it is not the pitching of the sea that is making Edmée sick. In terms of food, heat and oxygen, the conditions are right: it is with total indifference that the inevitable event occurs. The blood circulates, the sea is smooth, the Earth spins, and at both poles all is calm and white.